RAMPS DOWN, TROOPS AWAY

RAMPS DOWN, TROOPS AWAY

Duncan Harding

Severn House Large Print
London & New York

This first large print edition published in Great Britain 2005 by
SEVERN HOUSE LARGE PRINT BOOKS LTD of
9-15 High Street, Sutton, Surrey, SM1 1DF.
First world regular print edition published 2004 by
Severn House Publishers, London and New York.
This first large print edition published in the USA 2005 by
SEVERN HOUSE PUBLISHERS INC., of
595 Madison Avenue, New York, NY 10022.

British Library Cataloguing in Publication Data

Harding, Duncan, 1926 -
    Ramps down, troops away! : a novel of D-day. - Large print ed.
    1.   World War, 1939 – 1945 -
        Campaigns - France - Normandy - Fiction
    2.   War stories
    3.   Large type books
    I.   Title
    823.9'14 [F]

    ISBN 0-7278-7439-X

Printed and bound in Great Britain by
MPG Books Ltd, Bodmin, Cornwall.

'Twas on a summer's day – the sixth of June.
I like to be particular in dates.
They are a sort of post-house, where the Fates
Change horses, making history change its tune.

Lord Byron, Don Juan

They mark our passage as a race of men,
Earth will not see such ships as those again.

Masefield

Author's Note

You know me by now, gentle reader, don't you? Heart of gold, sucker for a sob story, always on the lookout for a good tale that'll please you (especially when there's money involved for yours truly). I don't care if my fellow writers – a lot of pinko puffs for the most part – call me 'Harding the Hack'. But sometimes even I can't take it.

It was when my publisher – public school and posh plonk – asked me to do a book on D-Day that this old hack's spirit sank into his sneakers. Not another book on that famous day in June 1944. Why, there's whole libraries full of 'em, not to mention the movies, especially those Yank ones where the GIs do all the fighting and the Brits sit down and have another tea break. *No, not D-Day!*

But what was I going to do? I needed the publisher's dosh, as pitiful as it is. That new girlfriend of mine – well she's not exactly a 'girl' – is expensive. I met her through the local rag. You know the lark: 'Women 4 Men'; all 'GSOH', 'OTT', 'TLC' sort of

7

thing. You need to be a bloody cryptographer to understand the ad in the first place. Anyhow, I needed the money for her; she doesn't half like her old 'G&Ts' (I swear she must have shares in Gordon's Gin, the way she knocks back the stuff, even after breakfast. Well, what with her and the rent for the hovel I live in, I was in need of the readies. So I accepted my publisher's generous offer, with cash in advance, mind you – publishers are a dodgy lot. So another D-Day book was born.

Funnily enough, when I got down to doing the research for the new book I found I quite liked the project. Naturally I knew something about D-Day. I'd always thought my dear old missing dad had taken part in it with the Pioneer Corps – 'The Royal Corps of Shit-Shovellers', as he used to call his unit in a joking manner. That was till I found out he'd deserted from the army after he'd got poor mum in the family way, and had spent most of 1944 on the trot, living off the earnings of an old bag from Burnley who was on the game somewhere down south. But that, gentle reader, is another story, to be revealed when the Harding family saga is finally released to an expectant western world.

Anyway, as I was saying, I started to get

interested in the whole murderous business of that June Tuesday sixty years ago. The numbers involved were staggering. Five thousand ships, mostly British, and over 150,000 assault troops, again more Brits than Yanks. Please note that, Mr Spielberg. But it wasn't really the numbers that grabbed me. It was the men, most of whom were going to die that sixth June.

There was the regular, Colonel Ferguson of the Royal Engineers. He'd done his bit already. But he still felt it his duty to have another go for the 'King-Emperor', as he would have called the poor old stuttering British monarch of the time. It cost him his life. Then there was 'Crazy Carl', the Jerry naval lieutenant, with his black bra flag and grotty stomach. He bought it, too. But, above all, I was taken by Charlie Seagram, a bit of a boozer like myself (how could he be otherwise with a name like 'Seagram'). Young Charlie Seagram seemed pretty typical of them all, doomed from the very start.

Good war till his wife took up with the Yanks. Then it was downhill all the way till he got his last chance on D-Day. He took it, of course. Young Brits were like that in those days, not full of piss and vinegar as they are today. He might have been scared, but he

9

was too frightened of what his comrades might think of him to show that he was. The inevitable happened, naturally. He bought it like some 10,000 other Brits, Yanks and Canucks before that 6th June 1944 was over.

But we haven't forgotten them altogether, thank God. Every year we celebrate their passing. There are military bands, po-faced bishops in frocks, 'celebrities', politicos hogging the TV cameras and hoping their make-up won't show, as they prepare for the next election.

Of course, the dead 'heroes' weren't a bit like the men we celebrate. Most of them hated the bullshit 'if it moves, salute it; if it don't, paint it white' sort of thing. They weren't too fond of parades either, especially church parades. And I doubt if they would have taken too kindly to politicians wearing lipstick and rouge. 'Bloody lot o' pansies,' they would have sneered.

All the same, although we don't have a real clue what those men sixty years ago were like, it is good that we haven't forgotten them. They deserve to be remembered. We'll never see their like again.

Duncan Harding, Caen, France 2003

BOOK ONE

A Boozer Becomes a Bigot

Shall we not sail against his territory? Where will we find a landing place? someone asks. The war itself will discover the weak places in his position.

Demosthenes

One

The morning was bright with the winter sunshine. The sun's rays held no warmth, yet they did give London's bomb-shattered buildings a mellow look. They fitted in with the rest of the wartime capital, as if most of it had fallen down into ruins a long time ago.

Lieutenant Seagram walked through the capital's streets purposefully, although as usual he had one hell of a head. But that was to be expected from a man who drank a bottle of whisky a day when he could afford it at black market prices. There were Allied servicemen everywhere: British, Americans, Poles, Frenchmen and half a dozen other nationalities he couldn't place. Few of them saluted him. But Seagram had got used to that. He wasn't the ideal officer type with his belly and shabby, salt-stained uniform. Even the Royal Naval matelots who passed him didn't salute if they could avoid it. After all, he was only an officer in the 'wavy navy', the Royal's naval reserve. Regulars didn't think much of such types.

Seagram touched the half bottle of Scotch which bulged from the left pocket of his tunic. He wished he dared unscrew it there and then to have a hefty swig. He needed the Dutch courage that the fiery spirit would give him. But he fought the temptation. It wouldn't look too good if he faced the admiral smelling of Scotch. He walked on.

Above him in the hard blue sky the barrage balloons sailed like silver slugs. Down below in the park to his left, ATS manning the anti-aircraft guns, surrounded by sandbags which still sparkled with hoar frost, the women gunners were going through their usual morning drills. GIs lazed at the gates, whistling every time one of the women bent down, exposing her khaki-clad rump. 'Americans!' Seagram told himself. 'All they think about is sex.' But the next moment the bitter look vanished from his mottled drinker's face. One day soon they'd get their comeuppance. Then the days of whistling at girls would be over and the bloody business of killing would commence.

He swung into Piccadilly, slowing his pace as he approached the Yanks' 'Rainbow Corner' club. Here no one walked in hurry, especially if you were a GI or a 'Piccadilly

Commando', as they called the whores. And there were plenty of both types about. It seemed to Seagram that half the US Army was to be on leave. There were GIs everywhere, jackets open, caps on the backs of their heads as they lounged against walls, chewing gum steadily like cows working their cud back and forth. 'Christ,' he told himself, 'they look as green as the growing corn. Do they really know what they're in for?' But there seemed to be no answer to that particular question.

A whore in a shabby summer frock wobbled towards him on heels that were too high for her. Her hair was uncombed and she might well have been a little drunk, too. She flashed him a false-toothed smile and said, voice slurred, 'Fancy a nice time, sailor? I'm cheap.'

Seagram couldn't help it. That old bitterness welled up inside him, the product of too much alcohol, failure and a hard war. 'Yes,' he said, 'and you look it, miss.'

'Frig you!' she snarled and turned away, heading unsteadily for the nearest GI, waggling her skinny rump, as if in contempt. Seagram smiled his twisted smile. Even if she had been attractive, he wouldn't have known what to do with her. The booze had taken its toll on that, too. It seemed an age since he had last had a woman. He shrugged slightly and passed on, wishing even more fervently now that he could stop in a doorway and take a swig out of his half bottle of Scotch. It wasn't to be, for now the two Yank military policemen guarding the door of the US club were eyeing him suspiciously, swinging their white-painted clubs more furiously, as if they were about to assault him at any moment. He knew why. He *did* look suspicious with his fat gut and shabby uniform, with a strip of fading medal ribbons on his chest. Nobody in his right mind would take him for a real naval officer, who was actually captain of a ship, rusty, expiring old tub that she was.

On the steps in between the two big MPs an old crone was sweeping the debris of the night before, singing *'There'll be bluebirds over the white cliffs of Dover'* tonelessly to herself. Suddenly she stopped in mid-verse and pulled what looked like a pair of knickers from the rubbish. She cackled with delight and held them up for the entertainment of the two MPs, who went red with embarrassment. 'What d' yer say to these, eh, soldier boys? Bet the tart who wore 'em last night lost more than her knickers, eh?'

16

And she cackled again until she started to cough, and the bigger of the military policemen snapped, 'Get on with your work, lady.'

Seagram passed on, followed by the old woman's wheezes and the brassy music of the 'One O'Clock Jump' coming from the club's amplifiers.

Now, as he turned into Shaftesbury Avenue, the street traffic thickened. London was going to work. The pavements were packed with middle-aged men. All of them were in the same sort of dress, as if it were a kind of uniform: shabby trenchcoat, bowler hat, gas mask slung over the shoulder by a piece of string, and, naturally, the furled umbrella, carried like a sword. The women seemed little different: headscarves and high heels, floral dresses under shabby coats that were obviously pre-war (no one had clothing coupons for coats these days). Even though it was a cold March day, most of them were bare legged, or had their legs painted brown with a carefully drawn black line down the calves, like a seam. Seagram sniffed. No wonder the GIs dangled nylons in front of the British women, as if they were the most precious gift in the world.

'London, spring 1944,' he told himself. A picture of a nation about to attempt the great invasion. He laughed softly and cynically, though there was no answering light in his bloodshot eyes. 'What a hope,' he said aloud to no one in particular, but no one was listening. No one ever did to Lieutenant Charles Seagram, DSC RNVR these days. He waddled on...

Somewhere in the basement of the shabby house which was the rendezvous, one of the matelots who guarded the place was singing, 'Ain't it a pity, she's only got one titty to feed the baby on ... Poor little bugger's got only one udder—' A harsh voice commanded, 'No more o' that, laddie, or I'll have ye on the rattle.' The singing stopped as if someone had suddenly slashed the unseen seaman's throat.

Seagram peered at the shabby front door and the nameplates. Once they had been polished brass. Now they were green and unpolished and it was difficult for him to make out the one he sought. 'Christ,' he said, talking to himself like a lonely man, 'you're going frigging blind as well.' He licked his dry lips. He'd give his left bollock for a stiff drink now, but even as he pressed the bell punch and the door began to creak open, he knew it was already too late for that. He'd have to face the brass sober. It was a terrible thought. A voice made him forget his thirst. It was one of authority, that of a man used to giving orders and having them obeyed – *at once.*

Peering a little in the gloom he saw the naval officer standing at the end of the smelly entrance corridor. He was evidently some kind of aide, for he wore the gold lanyard dangling from the shoulder of his elegant uniform. And even as he stood there, Seagram could smell the odour of the expensive cologne that the unknown officer used. 'Lieutenant Seagram?' the elegant aide snapped.

'Yessir,' Seagram answered, though he couldn't make out the rank of the officer standing there in the gloom. 'Reporting as ordered, sir.'

'Yes, of course. Follow me.' He turned and began to lead the way up the dirty stairs, which creaked at every step. Seagram did so, wondering why after all the cloak and-dagger stuff leading up to this rendezvous no one had asked for his naval identification card. But then it dawned on him that there would be others in the side rooms leading off from the rickety stairs, watching his every movement; it seemed that kind of place.

19

At the head of the stairs a light went on abruptly. It blinded Seagram for a moment. He blinked rapidly several times and told himself it had to be some sort of security device. What kind he didn't know. But whatever its purpose, his guide used it for a close inspection of him and his uniform. Almost disdainfully, his supercilious gaze rose from Seagram's scuffed, unpolished shoes, along the salt-stained, poorly pressed navy-blue trousers up to his tunic bulging over his belly and on to his battered white cap, its insignia tarnished and green.

It was obvious his guide didn't overly like what he saw, for he said, 'You do know, Seagram, don't you, that you're going to see an admiral?' He wrinkled his nose and sniffed, as if he had just smelled something putrid and rotten. 'Bit of shit order, if you ask me, Seagram.'

Hastily Seagram bit his tongue to prevent one of his bitter comments, for he sensed this surprise summons to meet an admiral at a secret rendezvous in London might mean a change in his lacklustre career of the past two years when 'it' had happened. Ever since then he had been virtually on the beach, and he was heartily sick of it. He hadn't volunteered for the wavy navy back

20

in '39 to haul Yankee liberty ships, probably laden with cargoes of french letters for randy GIs, into Liverpool harbour. So he contented himself with, 'Sorry, Lieutenant, but on the kind of old tub I command up north, shit order is customary. Conditions are rough.'

Again the aide sniffed. 'I suppose so, Seagram, but I'd advise, with your record – you know what I mean?' – his gaze bored into the other man's flabby, mottled face – 'that you behave yourself. You might hear something favourable if you do. All right, end of sermon. Here we go.' He knocked on the door to his left and, without waiting to be called in, opened it and entered.

Seagram succumbed. The tension was too great. After the years of disgrace and humiliation, this mysterious summons to London, where as the snotty-nosed aide with his cut-glass accent had hinted he might hear 'something favourable' if he toed the line, was too much for him to bear any longer. He didn't hesitate. He pulled out the flask and, not taking his eyes off the closed door for an instant, he raised the bottle of Haig – *'Don't be vague – order Haig'* – to his lips. He took a great gulp. Instantly he felt the fiery warmth of the Scotch surge through his body.

'Christ, that hit the spot all right,' he wheezed, and then, just as the door started to open again, he thrust the bottle back into his pocket and stood there like an embarrassed schoolboy caught by a master pulling his plonker in the lavs.

Again the aide sniffed. He appeared to sniff at regular intervals. Then he looked hard at Seagram, who avoided his gaze. He felt he looked as guilty as hell. In a world full of arseholes who didn't drink, he always felt out of place – guilty. It was better not to challenge the holier-than-thou sods, even with a look. The aide said, 'The admiral will see you now. And remember, Seagram, watch your p's and q's.'

'Thank you, I will,' he ground out the words through gritted teeth, his wet fists clenched with anger. He would have dearly loved to have punched the snotty-nosed twerp in the kisser. But he didn't dare. Perhaps this was going to be his last chance, and he wasn't going to risk it now.

The aide opened the door again. A knife of bright white light stabbed the gloomy corridor. 'He's here, sir,' the aide announced and stood to one side to let Seagram enter.

Bracing his shoulders, as if he were back in the training school, Lieutenant Seagram entered, blinking a little in the bright light. 'Lieutenant Seagram, First—' he began. But his words were drowned by a great booming hearty voice from the past, which chortled, 'Good – *bloody* good – to see you, Charlie!'

He swayed as if he might fall, totally caught by surprise at the sight of the great hulk of an admiral advancing towards him from his desk, his big paw outstretched. At that moment he looked as if he might well tear Seagram's right arm off.

'Holy frigging cow ... You, Bert!' Seagram stuttered, totally overwhelmed by the big sailor with his upwards curled and waxed eyebrows and great black mass of a beard. 'Well, I'll be buggered.'

'Well, it's up to you, Charlie,' the admiral boomed in that great loud voice which, when he had commanded his cruiser, had made many a frightened snotty fill his pants.

Seagram caught hold of himself. 'Sorry, Bert ... er, Admiral,' he floundered. 'I was caught off—'

Admiral Challenger gave Seagram a massive bear-hug which must have broken at least two of the younger officer's ribs and roared, 'Forget the admiral, old chap – *old shipmate*,' and in the very next breath he called over Seagram's shoulder to the astonished aide, 'Well, Blenkinsop, don't just stand there like a spare prick at a wedding. Get us some coffee and see it's bloody well laced with Nelson's blood.'

'*Rum*, sir?' Blenkinsop gasped. 'But it's only ten o'clock in the morning.'

'As late as that,' the admiral bellowed, delighted by the shocked look on his aide's face. 'Well, then I think, Charlie, old shipmate, we'll need a double draught of old Nelson's blood. Come on, Blenkinsop, chop, chop, let's get to it. It's not every day I meet an old shipmate like Lieutenant Seagram here. We don't want to make this into a lash-up, do we, Blenkinsop? Move it!'

The elegant aide 'moved it', his golden lanyard swinging wildly to and fro in his agitation like an acrobat's swing. The rum did the trick. Suddenly, startlingly, for the first time in the long dreary winter months of 1943–44, Lieutenant Seagram felt happy again. Perhaps it wasn't only 'Nelson's blood' that had done the trick. Perhaps it was the presence of his old shipmate Bert Challenger, who had made this surprise appearance in the shabby house in the guise of an admiral, not just a rear admiral, but a real admiral, one who seemed to have impressive powers. For now, after the mixture

24

of hot coffee and rum had begun to have its effect, he said to his old friend, 'Charlie, I'll have your guts for garters if you ever blab about what I'm going to tell you now.'

'Scout's honour,' Seagram swore with unaccustomed lightness, raising his fingers as if he were about to swear an oath.

'Good show, old chap. I knew I could trust you when they showed me the list of available and able officers.'

Seagram was not so tipsy that he asked what list his old shipmate was referring to. Instead he said, 'Fire away, Bert. Give me the good news. I know I don't damn well deserve it. But in God's name, I bloody well need it.'

For a moment the admiral looked at his old shipmate long and hard. He could have sworn he saw the glint of tears in Seagram's bloodshot drunk's eyes, then he dismissed the notion. Charlie Seagram was too hard an old hand to be teary and sentimental. He put his big arm around Seagram's shoulders and whispered, almost as if he didn't want the supercilious aide Blenkinsop to hear. 'Old shipmate, I'm going to let you into a great secret. Come into the next room. I want to introduce you to somebody. Then I'll make you a bigot.'

Totally dazed, not even able to enquire what in hell's name a 'bigot' was, Charlie Seagram let himself be led into the next room.

Two

'Colonel Ferguson,' the admiral announced as the tall slim officer, bent over what appeared to Seagram to be a sand table, straightened up and turned round.

He flashed the two naval officers a brilliant smile, though his bronzed face remained hard and careful. Seagram took in the deep tan and the ribbons of the 'Africa Star' and the Military Cross on the army officer's chest and told himself that Ferguson had to be one of the battle-experienced desert officers that Montgomery had brought back to England with him the previous January to stiffen up the mostly green British troops who would carry out the coming invasion of France.

Hastily the admiral introduced the two men, the one fat and flabby, the other hard

26

and lean with not an ounce of surplus fat on his body. Then he got down to business immediately. Leading a puzzled Seagram to the sand table, he said without any further preliminaries, 'Well, Charlie. This is it. This is where we're going to invade Hitler's *Festung Europa* – European Fortress to you, old shipmate.'

Seagram gasped as if someone had just punched him hard in his fat gut. He had just been let into the greatest secret of the war, one that millions of people all over the free world had been lusting to have revealed to them for years now: where the Allies were going to land.

The admiral smiled, and Ferguson did the same, only more hesitantly, as if he were weighing Seagram up, wondering if he were not perhaps the right person to be given such privileged information. 'So you're now a bigot, Charlie,' the admiral smiled. 'And there must be no more than a thousand of us, Allied officers included, who know the great secret. Even the King-Emperor doesn't. That devil Monty,' he meant the British army commander, General Bernard Montgomery, the Victor of El Alamein, 'wouldn't give permission for the King to be told. No matter.' He looked at the army

27

man. 'Ferguson here, of the Royal Engineers, will explain the details. I'll be in the main office.' He looked hard at his old shipmate as if he were seeing him for the very first time and was trying to assess him. 'I want a word with you before you leave.' And with that he was gone, striding to the door, as if he were still on the quarterdeck of the cruiser he had lately commanded before a German U-boat had torpedoed it in the Med.

Just like the admiral, the Royal Engineer colonel didn't waste any further time. He took up the pointer lying on the sand table and pointed to a stretch of coastline, flanked by high papier-mâché cliffs and set between two rivers. Both rivers, the cliffs and the surrounding coastal villages were all clearly labelled with their French names. Here, in this tiny office in this run-down shabby house, the whole plan of the British part of the great invasion was clearly revealed. Seagram licked his suddenly dry lips and asked himself why a broken-down bastard of a wavy navy officer such as he was was being let into this tremendous secret.

But at the moment Ferguson was not about to enlighten him. Instead, with the clipped precision of a regular army officer, which he clearly was, he launched into his exposé. 'There you are,' he exclaimed, extending his hands like a conjuror who has just produced a white rabbit from a top hat. 'Our corps's objective. This stretch of beach between the River Orne – here – and the River Seulles – here.' He tapped the sand table with his pointer. 'Our objective for the first day of the invasion – D+1, is the code name for it – is to capture the city of Caen – there! It is vital we do so, for it's a rail and road junction, and once the bastards of the 12th SS Division get established there we'll have one hell of a job winkling them out. Tough little buggers.'

Seagram nodded his understanding, but said nothing. He was still in a state of mild shock at the amazing change in his circumstances. Too, at the back of his mind, there was a growing feeling of unease. Whatever this 'bigot' business had to do with him, he knew it would place hellish pressure on him. The question was, would he be able to cope?

'Now, the task of capturing Caen is to be given to Monty's old division – the one he took to France before that bloody fiasco at Dunkirk – the Third Infantry Division.' Ferguson gave Seagram a tight little smile.

'They call it the Iron Division, but just how solid the iron will be is anyone's guess. The Division hasn't fired a shot since 1940. They've spent the last four years training – and training, as you know, Seagram, is slightly different from the real thing when somebody's shooting back at you.'

'The opposition?' Ferguson answered his own question. 'Not so strong, once the Third clears the beach. Intelligence says it consists of three battalions of the Boche 716 Division, plus several battalions of Russians, Poles, Ukrainians and the like, all former Red Army men who volunteered – out of hunger – to leave their POW camps and fight for the Boche.'

'Now,' Ferguson tapped the model like a schoolmaster trying to attract the attention of his pupils, although Seagram doubted whether, with his fierce demeanour, he would have had any trouble with unruly kids, 'the two lead battalions coming from the sea will be the Iron Division's East Yorks, going in here, and the South Lancs, here. There they'll be up against the right bank of the River Orne.' He paused momentarily, as if he had suddenly lost the thread. Then he picked it up again, but this time his voice was no longer as confident or incisive.

Indeed, Seagram sensed he had come to a problem of some kind that concerned him. He leaned forward more attentively.

'But there's a problem. One week ago, aerial recce discovered that there's a bunker right in the path of the South Lancs, some hundred yards or so from where their landing barges will hit the beach. All the other bunkers we've targeted can be dealt with by the RAF or the Royal Navy firing off-shore. But this one can't.' He paused again as if he had just realized for the first time the seriousness of the problem.

'Commandos?' Seagram suggested.

Ferguson shook his head. 'We've thought of it. No deal. They'd be mown down before they'd gone a dozen yards. The outer defences of the bloody place are alive with MGs. Besides, they've got a minefield all around the bunker. No, that's not the answer.'

'I am, then,' Seagram said bluntly, realizing now why he had been brought here, but not knowing exactly what use his old tub would be in a land operation of this kind.

'Yes, I suppose you could say that,' Ferguson answered thoughtfully. 'Though if I were in your shoes, Lieutenant, it's not a job I'd volunteer for, what.'

'But I didn't. I was called.'

31

'Then someone – perhaps the admiral – is volunteering your services without your advance knowledge.' He looked at Seagram's raddled drinker's face and pot belly a little sadly, almost as if he pitied the naval officer. 'Anyway, this is what's planned for you and your ship—' But Ferguson didn't finish his explanation. for in that same instant, as the sirens to the east began to wail, a harsh official broke in with 'Jerry's overhead! Everyone out ... down to the shelters in the basement ... Move it, now ... EVERYONE OUT!'

It was one of the new German 'tip-and-run' raids. The enemy would come in low over the south coast, avoiding the local radar, and then sweep in at tree-top height for the capital, hoping to drop their bombs and be away before Fighter Control could scramble its planes and the anti-aircraft batteries, scattered all over London, could take up the challenge. Such raids couldn't be compared with the great attacks of 1940–41 when hundreds of Londoners were killed or maimed night after night for four months. But all the same they kept the civilians on edge, breaking into their sleep, making the war-weary populace, existing on poor rations, ever more exhausted.

These attacks didn't affect Seagram. He was used to them – and worse. Still, in the dim light of the house's cellars, packed with sailors and what he took to be Admiralty civvies, he felt the occasion was a good opportunity to take a swig from the bottle of Haig resting temptingly in his pocket. People often did drink in shelters to calm their nerves. But something made him desist.

He guessed it might be something to do with the great secret that he had just been let into, now that he was a 'bigot', whatever the hell that name stood for! Too, he felt he was being given a second chance after all these years – a chance to 'redeem' himself, as his dear old Catholic mother Bridget would have said. Wasn't that perhaps why Bert, now an admiral, had picked him out of no-where to be given some sort of important job in the coming invasion? Bert knew his record. Indeed, as a lieutenant commander back in '42 when it had all begun, he had been there right at the start. He patted his pocket to reassure himself that the half bottle was still there, in case he needed it, and then took his hand away as if he had just touched something red hot. For Ferguson, followed by the admiral's aide, Blenkinsop, was pushing his way down the corridor of the shelter, which was now turning blue in the poor yellow light with the smoke of scores of cheap Woodbines and Capstan cigarettes that the matelots were smoking as the bombs thundered outside and tiny particles of whitewash came floating down from the ceiling like early snow.

Ferguson plumped himself down beside Seagram, a briefcase, marked 'secret', tied to his left wrist by a chain. Blenkinsop remained standing. 'Sorry about that,' the colonel said. 'One of those things, eh. We'll continue the briefing once I can arrange a new meeting with his nibs, Bert to you, Admiral to me.' He flashed Seagram a white-toothed smile and suddenly Seagram realized he had found an ally in the lean, sun-tanned soldier, albeit perhaps a critical one. Still, it felt good to know that people were beginning to regard him seriously once more. He said, 'Well I've known him a long time, Colonel, you know. Off and on since '39, to be exact. We were at Dunkirk together, too.'

Ferguson nodded indulgently, as if the rumpled fat naval officer was talking about ancient history.

Blenkinsop, the dutiful aide, couldn't contain himself any longer. 'The admiral's compliments, gentlemen.' He looked from Ferguson to Seagram and the latter could not suppress a smile; now he was included among the 'gentlemen'. It was obvious that the fact he could address Blenkinsop's boss as 'Bert' had left an impression on the foppish twit with his bloody gold lanyard.

'Yes?' Ferguson said.

'Bit of a flap on at the Admiralty. The admiral excuses himself. He'll be in touch again as soon as possible. But, Colonel,' he addressed the army officer directly, 'everything is to go on as scheduled, sir.'

'Thank you,' Ferguson said, as outside in the far distance the first of the air raid sirens started to sound the all-clear. The enemy fighter-bombers were finishing their tip-and-run raid, and beginning to race back across the Channel to their bases in France. Ferguson sighed. 'North Africa was never as bad as this. At least up the blue' – the Western Desert – 'a man could get a bit of kip at night. That was a gentleman's war.'

He rose and held out his hand again. Seagram took it. It was cold and steady; it was the hand, Seagram guessed, of a man who had never been frightened for a single moment in his whole life. 'I'll be in touch, Seagram – soon.' He took one last hard look at Seagram, as if he were attempting to etch his face on to his mind's eye for eternity, then, putting on his cap, he started to push his way out of the smelly cellar. For the first time, Seagram noted that he limped badly, favouring his right side, and now he could hear the audible squeak of an artificial leg. Ferguson was yet another casualty of the war as was Seagram himself. The soldier had lost a limb; he had lost his reputation and self-respect. For a moment he wondered which was worse. Then Blenkinsop spoke once more.

'The admiral told me to tell you one thing, Seagram,' he said, sounding slightly puzzled.

'And what was that, Lieutenant?' Seagram asked absently.

'He said, "Remember the *Curacoa*." ' The aide frowned. 'Mean anything to you, Seagram?'

Seagram didn't reply. He couldn't. Every time he heard that word it was like a fatal stab to the heart by a very sharp knife. It seemed to take his very breath away. He waved a hand vaguely in front of his face as if trying to remove something there which was impeding his vision.

More puzzled than ever, Blenkinsop looked at Seagram and told himself he'd heard the fat down-at-heel skipper was given to drink. Perhaps he'd been knocking the booze back while he was in the shelter; he'd already noted the bulge of the bottle in the lieutenant's pocket. He told himself the boss, the admiral, had some very peculiar friends for a senior naval officer. Aloud he said, 'Well, I'll be cutting along now. The all-clear's sounding overhead now.' He touched his hand perfunctorily to his elegant cap and turned. 'Goodbye then, Seagram.'

The latter didn't appear to hear. He continued to stare into space, as the noisy young sailors started to leave, nipping out their precious cigarettes and placing the fag ends carefully behind their right ears in flagrant disobedience of King's Regulations.

Somehow Seagram found himself outside, carried there probably by the flood of excited young sailors. Now the blood-red ball hung in the hard blue sky, supported, it seemed, by the black columns of smoke rising slowly in the windless morning. Still Seagram appeared not to notice, nor to see anything in fact. His mind was too full of that dread name: *Curacoa ... His Majesty's Light Cruiser Curacoa! God,* he choked to himself, would he ever be freed of that name and that memory?

He didn't care. He needed a drink. He waited till the last of the young sailors had pushed by him, crossing over the debris-littered road, dodging the ambulances, bells jingling, on their way to the nearest incident, on their way to the mobile canteen which had appeared out of nowhere. Then, leaning against the brick wall, he took out his bottle. He didn't even attempt to conceal it. With hands that trembled badly now, he raised it to his lips.

Holding it with both hands, fearful that he might drop it, he took a deep draught of the Scotch. Almost immediately he felt the fiery burn of the whisky going down his gullet. His trembling ceased almost immediately. He breathed out hard and suddenly felt ashamed of himself. Hurriedly he put the bottle back into his hip pocket, but not quickly enough. A child passing hand in hand with his mother, the iron curlers peering out from the flowered turban she wore, cried in a loud voice, 'Mummy ... Mummy. Look at that sailor drinking. Is he drunk?'

Three

It had started with Churchill, to be exact, in a scrambled telephone conversation across the Atlantic between the British Prime Minister and General George Marshall, the Head of the US Chiefs of Staff. For a while, the two men, one half American, the other a full-blooded Virginian whose highest priority was the honour of the US Army, talked about the use of the two *Queens* as means of transport for the first American troops to come to Britain to take part in the invasion of Europe.

The two *Queens*, the *Queen Mary* and the *Queen Elizabeth*, both 80,000 tonners and the pride of the British Merchant Navy and the populace as a whole (for their construction in the mid-thirties had symbolized Britain coming out of the Depression), had now been offered by Churchill to the US Army. It was a very generous offer, for if one of the German submarine 'wolf-packs' sank one of the *Queens* it would be a tremendous blow to British pride; the Germans would hail it as a major victory.

Now, this summer of 1942, Marshall was suggesting that the *Queens* should be employed to ferry thousands of US fighting men to Britain.

And he was asking the Prime Minister a difficult question. Over the transatlantic link, the line full of strange bubbles and creaks, as if at several thousand fathoms weird deepsea monsters were taking their pleasure, he asked, 'Sir, how many men would you suggest we put aboard one of the *Queens*?'

'You know, Marshall,' Churchill answered slowly, knowing that not even the President of the United States dare address the Chief of Staff by his first name, 'the *Queens* have only enough lifeboats and rafts for some eight thousand men.'

'I know, Prime Minister,' Marshall said. 'But if we disregarded the pre-war maritime safety regulations we could ship twice that number to the UK. Say sixteen thousand troops, the equivalent of a whole infantry division.'

The thought of a whole US infantry division being sent to Britain with each of the *Queens* cheered Churchill up considerably. It would be a tonic for the hard-pressed British people, who had suffered defeat after defeat in these last two years, to know that the 'Yanks' were arriving in divisional strength every time a *Queen* docked in Liverpool or Belfast. All the same, the risk was considerable. How would the Great American Public react, if a *Queen* were sunk by one of *Gross-admiral* Doenitz's damned U-boats with a huge loss of life, with the US Press reporting as it would that there hadn't been sufficient lifeboats and floats for all the troops carried by the British liners? Churchill could guess. Yet once again he was faced by one of those overwhelming moral decisions with which he was confronted almost daily this summer.

For once the Grand Old Man did not give a clear-cut decision. Instead, he told the hard-faced US general, 'I can only tell you, Marshall, what we would do. We wouldn't take the risk of not having enough lifeboats and floats. You must evaluate the risk yourself, I'm afraid, and then make your decision.'

There was a pause. Over that three thousand mile long undersea cable, Churchill, puffing slowly at his cigar, imagined he could almost hear the US general thinking over the problem. Then it came. Marshall said in that slow Virginian drawl of his, 'OK, Prime Minister, we'll do it your way for a start. We'll sail with a safe load – enough lifeboats to take the soldiers aboard to safety if – God forbid – the *Queen* is torpedoed. If that works, we'll fill 'em to the brim, sir.'

'Splendid, General!' Churchill chortled happily. It was the decision he had hoped for and it hadn't come from him. If anything went wrong, it would be on an American's head, not on his. After all, he knew just how delicate the Anglo-American relationship was even after the two countries had been allies for over six months. A recent US poll, sent to him by the British ambassador in Washington, showed that sixty per cent of all Yanks polled thought of Britain as an untrustworthy imperialist power. 'Remember, the *Queens* can do over thirty knots, twice the speed of any U-boat even if the Hun is on the surface. With only a mere sliver of luck, the *Queens* can outrun any Hun trying to attack them in the Atlantic crossing.'

Churchill thought he heard Marshall breathe in sharply, and he could guess why he had done so. A moment later the general said, 'You mean the *Queens* can go faster than any Jerry attempting to attack them? But where would that put their escorts, sir?

42

The older US Navy destroyers can't achieve speeds over thirty knots, I'm afraid.'

Churchill took a hard puff at his cigar. 'There is only one way to deal with the problem, General,' he said, somewhat ponderously for him. 'Single ship convoys.'

'Single ship!' Marshall echoed.

'Yes, relying on the *Queens*' superior speed, they'll just have to chance crossing the Atlantic by themselves without escorts. Anyway, Marshall, a typical convoy – escorts, supply ships and the rest of it – would slow them down and make them an obvious target for any U-boat commander worth his salt. They're so big they'd stand out like a sore thumb. They'd draw the Hun's attention immediately. Why waste a torpedo on a destroyer or tanker when you can hit one of the world's greatest ships? Mr Hitler would shower any such Hun with more medals than Marshal Goering.' Churchill chuckled.

Marshall didn't share his humour. He said, 'Single ship convoys, hmm.'

Churchill said, 'It does work. We sent the *Queen Mary* over in '40 without an escort. We simply relied on her speed.'

'Yessir,' Marshall objected. 'That was '40. Things have changed since then, sir. Those Jerry wolf-packs have gotten ever more cunning.'

Churchill nodded, but kept quiet. He knew all about U-boats. During the previous winter they had been sinking so much British tonnage bringing in food and supplies that the Mother Country had almost been on its knees, with supplies of flour and other essentials extending for only four short weeks.

'For example, sir, once these great ships of yours get close to the British ports, they have to reduce speed drastically.'

'Yes?'

'Well, we've had the same problem at our East Coast ports, Boston, New York and the like. There these Kraut wolf-packs have sunk our ships at will when they've been approaching the harbour at slow speed. Couldn't the enemy do the same thing at your ports, sir?'

'They could, but they don't in British coastal waters. We had the same problem for a short while in late '39, General. But as soon as I was recalled as First Sea Lord, I made immediately sure that when vessels approached our ports there would be a reception committee of smaller naval craft to escort them in and ensure that they weren't attacked by the enemy when they were at their most vulnerable, travelling at slow speeds. And let me assure you, General, the system worked and still does today. Send us your young soldiers and you can rest assured that no harm will come to them in British waters.' It was a proud boast, but the Grand Old Man would regret the day he made it. For it was to cost not the lives of Marshall's GIs, but those of many hundreds of honest British sailors.

That summer of 1942, when Churchill and Marshall instigated the 'single ship' convoy system, everything went exactly as Churchill had promised. By the end of that summer, the last one of Britain's defeats, over twenty fast 'single ship' convoys reached Britain. They carried hundreds of thousands of American troops safely across the submarine-infested waters of the Atlantic.

Indeed, by the end of that summer there were already two whole US divisions in Ireland alone and another one on its way, with a total of nearly two hundred thousand American GIs beginning to spread from Northern Ireland to the British mainland, where they would train for the next two years for the invasion of France that would come one day.

45

The flotilla of destroyers and motor boats covered by fighters from the British coastal land bases, preceded by lone Sunderland flying boats of Coastal Command, would sweep out from the Clyde or whatever the port area assigned to the *Queens* coming in from the States, throwing a protective net over a hundred miles or so. Ratings at their asdics, high flying coastal observers and low-flying Spitfire pilots would all be intent on spotting the first of a German wolf-pack: six or seven lean, deadly U-boats abreast, waiting to pounce on the *Queen* like some predatory wolf on its fat quarry. Time and time again the planes would disperse or destroy the enemy craft so that the great ship could sail majestically into port with the bands playing, the dockers cheering and thousands of pale-faced GIs, still sea-sick or sickened by British stewed mutton and boiled cabbage for breakfast, staring down at the dock so far below in wonder, as if they couldn't quite believe that they had made it safely after all.

As Churchill told a secret session of Parliament just before the great victory of El Alamein in the Western Desert, 'Gentlemen, thanks to our senior service and those fine types of the Merchant Navy who serve under our battered red duster, we are bringing the United States of America into this war in full force. Just as they did in 1918, our cousins from over the sea will re-dress the balance in our favour. Together we will win this war.' There were many present in the bombed House of Commons that day who were not convinced about 'our cousins from over the sea', but they cheered all the same...

But those rendezvous with the approaching *Queens* out in the U-boat-infested seas off the coast of Britain took their toll on the men of the 'senior service', who sailed out in all weathers and under uncertain conditions to protect the great ships packed with their human cargoes. And it wasn't just the fear of the unseen enemy lurking beneath the grey-green sea that wore the crews down and sometimes broke their nerve, it was the hardship, the long hours, the same old rations, the lack of privacy, the days when even the hardest old sweat couldn't keep his food down for more than an hour, as their frail craft bucked and heaved in the wild winter seas – with, as their only consolation of a day broken into four-hour watches, a hastily snatched kip in a warm bunk just vacated by another matelot going on duty

47

and a tot of breath-catching rum.

Off duty, things weren't much better for the young sailors. For those who were HO (hostilities only) men, who were signed up solely for the duration of the war and who were mostly single, there were the cheap whores of the ports – the 'hoors', as they called them. They would give them a 'five bob knee trembler' against the wall of the nearest air raid shelter. The women, often toothless and old before their time, believed that if you did it standing up you didn't need a 'french letter' because you couldn't get pregnant that way.

For the older men, mostly from the south, there were the long journeys in crowded troop trains to London and then on to Portsmouth and Plymouth to see their wives and kids; trips that might take up to a day or even more if the lines had been bombed, and which they spent drinking and playing cards. For it was drink in the end that became the only real solace of the old regular petty officers and the 'three-stripers', the veterans who kept the 'senior service' going under such miserable conditions. Most of them were 'half seas over' much of the time, somehow managing to carry out their duties even though they saw everything through a haze of alcohol.

The younger officers, especially if they weren't regulars with a naval career to pursue, were little different. The volunteers of the wavy navy, who had been torn from the comforts of civilian life and weren't used to the hardships of the regular navy joined by boys aged thirteen, were worse. They fell into the same alcoholic trap. How could it be otherwise? Drink dulled their feelings, their longings, their desire for another life than this of the eternal green-grey heaving cold sea, the endless misery of the long patrols, the damp stench of their fellow humans, huddled together in wet proximity: an existence in which they didn't have a single moment of privacy even when they went to the stinking nauseating 'heads'. *

It was, therefore, not surprising that Charlie Seagram, the lower-middle-class city clerk with his minor public school education and his weekends messing about in boats on the Solent, indulging in a rather upper-crust hobby which he couldn't afford (especially when he married his Mavis on the eve of war, when he volunteered immediately for the wavy navy), gradually

* *ships' lavatories*

49

succumbed to the alcohol culture of the little ships, too. With him it had started late. Winning the Distinguished Service Cross at Dunkirk in 1940 had made him ambitious – for a while. There was talk that he should become a regular and perhaps train to go into submarines. For a while he was attached to a destroyer squadron based at Harwich, where most of the officers were regulars. There he had started to pick up their ways and mannerisms, even as far as the way they dressed, with that studied elegance of the regular: civvie 'bags' and public school scarves wrapped round their necks instead of the regulation collar and tie. The only trouble was that no one seemed to recognize his public school's colours.

By 1941 Dunkirk and his DSC had been forgotten and he was transferred from the posh destroyer squadron to the RN Patrol Service; it seemed that their Lordships of the Admiralty in their great wisdom were worried about the growing number of wavy navy chaps flooding the regular navy ships. It had to be stopped.

So by his third year of war Charlie was serving with has beens who had failed somewhere along the line, commanding ships crewed by raw HO men and hardened deep-

50

sea fishermen from ports such as Fleetwood, who didn't stand much nonsense and weren't impressed by officers who had supposedly learned their craft by 'mucking about in boats' on the Solent of a weekend.

It was then that he started to take more than the daily rum ration in order to relieve the boredom of minesweeping operations and the occasional seaborne rescue of some RAF bomber crew that had 'ditched' after a raid on Germany. The evening 'nip' began to become the morning 'nip', stolen surreptitiously from a half bottle of black market whisky. By the end of that hard, boring year he was drinking off and on most of the day, and it didn't help that his skipper would be confined to his cabin for days on end when they were at sea, due to his chronic ulcers; ulcers which turned out to be bottles of rum stolen from the wardroom pantry.

And then had come the trouble with Mavis.

Four

'Did I get a load of her beaver, buddy,' the big Yank major was saying to his friend, puffing heartily at his cigar. 'And boy was it parted in the middle. I could have gotten down on my hands and knees and eaten that pussy on the spot.' He laughed heartily, as did his companion. 'Brother, these English broads aren't the cool English roses I thought they were.'

Seagram stood to one side as they came up the steps of the basement club into the blackout, looking very pleased with themselves in a kind of well-fed, nothing's-going-to-hurt-me manner that ruffled the naval officer even more.

That day he had travelled all the way from the Clyde to London in a crowded train that seemed to stop at every station, large and small, to the capital, crouched most of the time in the lavatory next to a buxom ATS handing back and forth squalling babies who needed to be changed. As he remarked

52

to the woman, who had begun to smell of baby urine when finally the 'express' started to pull into King's Cross, 'We deserve a medal for this, miss.' To which she sighed in reply, 'And a very, very large G and T.'

And when he arrived at their flat he felt that he, too, could do with a 'very, very large G and T', for Mavis, who should have been there waiting for him, wasn't home. Instead, all he found in a flat that smelled of a strange but expensive perfume, was a hastily pencilled note reading, 'Gone to the Kit Kat. Be home late. Don't wait up for me.' She'd placed a single 'X' underneath the scribble, but hadn't, in her hurry, signed it.

For a few moments he had been bewildered. What was the Kit Kat? Why should Mavis, who had his old job in the insurance company, be going out at this time of the evening after a hard day's work, especially when she knew he was coming home on a seventy-two-hour pass? Christ, she hadn't seen him for three months. What was so important about this Kit Kat place?

His bewilderment had turned to anger, especially when he had followed the buxom smelly ATS's advice and found the gin. Normally Mavis didn't drink much more than a shandy or the occasional Babycham on special occasions; the gin she left to him. Now, however, the bottle was half empty, and there was no tonic. Had she had visitors who liked gin? he had asked himself, as he'd poured himself a neat one and downed it in one go.

Ten o'clock had come and gone. Outside the streets were silent. Most people would be in bed at this hour, he had told himself, especially as so many of them were working a sixty-hour week and had other duties on top of that like fire-watching, the Home Guard and the like.

By ten thirty he had finished the rest of the gin. Mavis had still not come. His worry about her absence had turned to anger once again, and by eleven he was outside, hailing the only taxi he could find, pressing a pound note into the cabbie's hand and commanding thickly, 'Take me to the Kit Kat, will you, cabbie.'

'Yessir,' the cabbie had replied cheerfully. 'But it'll be another five bob, sir.' Adding before Seagram could protest, 'It's worth the extra to get you in, sir. At this time of night the place is full of you young officers out on the razzle, if you know what I mean, sir.' And in the dim blue light the cabbie had winked at him knowingly.

Seagram hadn't known what he meant, but already he had decided that all was not as it should be with Mavis and that he was in for a surprise, whatever it might be.

He was right.

The Kit Kat, it was clear to him now, as the two American officers passed him on the stairs, was a peacetime drinking club, operating after hours, which had become a nightclub as soon as the big-spending Yanks had started to arrive in large numbers in the capital. As he pushed aside the blackout curtain to be greeted by a thick fug of blue cigarette smoke and a record of the Andrews Sisters belting out 'Boogie-Woogie Bugle Boy of Company B', he knew he was in one of those places he'd heard about from other young officers 'out on the razzle', which served expensive drinks and supplied cheap whores to the Yanks. But what in hell's name was Mavis doing in such a place? Was she working there as a waitress or something to make some spare cash? She'd not mentioned any such job to him. Indeed, in her infrequent letters – 'Darling, I'm just too tired to write every week' – she was always complaining about the workload of the job she had already.

He blinked in the smoke, and, standing

there a little helplessly in his stained, rumpled uniform, he searched the crowded noisy room for any sign of his wife. But even before his eyes had become accustomed to the dim red light, a waiter was at his side, urging, 'This way, sir. I have a seat free at a table with some other naval gentlemen. Very good, very good seat, you can see everything very good.' The waiter held out his right hand. Automatically, hardly aware that he was doing so, Seagram took out a half a crown and gave it to the dark-skinned waiter, who flashed him a smile, but not a very large one. Obviously the tip wasn't generous enough.

Moments later he found himself squeezed in between a very drunk lieutenant commander and an old lieutenant who looked as if he might have come up from the lower deck. The latter was saying, 'I had a bit of the other on a hillside once, Jack. Hard ferking graft, I can tell yer, screwing uphill. In the end, though, I got me bearing. I swung her arse a hundred and eighty degrees to port and banged away at her till her frigging glassy orbits nearly popped out of their sockets. Ha, ha!'

'Jack', the lieutenant commander, wasn't impressed. 'At my age, Bill, I prefer 'em on

56

top. Not so much hard work.' He patted his ample belly, while Seagram stared at the two of them as if they were creatures from another world. What was this Kit Kat place whose patrons were mainly men, middle-aged ones at that, concerned, it seemed, only with sex?

'Jack' thrust his belly upwards to make his point quite clear. It was as if he were balancing a woman on it. 'Then the gash can do the hard work. Walk ... trot ... canter ... and then *gallop*, if you follow me, Bill.' The lieutenant commander winked drunkenly at his companion and took another swallow of his drink, though most of the liquid ran down his fat jowls.

'You've got a wicked way with the wenches, Jack,' Bill said. 'I bet you could tell some juicy tales if—'

Suddenly he stopped short, as the greasy haired dark faced waiter who had shown a bemused Seagram to the table stepped up to a microphone at the front of the room, tapped it a couple of times and then said in a voice that he probably supposed was seductive, 'Now, gentlemen, can we have a little quiet, *please*?'

His response was a series of catcalls, raspberries and cries of 'Get off ... get off and bring on the tarts!'

The waiter's smile grew even broader; obviously he was used to such interruptions. *'Ple-ase*, gentlemen!' He extended his hands above his head like a promoter at a boxing match. 'Let us have applause now for *les girls.*' Smartly he stepped to one side, as from the curtain at the end of the crowded room *'les girls'* started to emerge, one by one, followed by a spotlight which made their teeth gleam with unnatural whiteness. It seemed to Seagram, as bemused as ever still, that they were the only things that gleamed in *'les girls'*, who, for the most part, appeared to be either sluts straight off the back streets or housewives who had put too much effort into their make-up – and what cheap tawdry underwear they were wearing!

'Now, gentlemen,' the waiter cried above the racket coming from the drunken officers, 'remember to note the girls' numbers. If you wish them to come to your table, there will be a small service charge and the cost of a drink for the little darlings.' He winked knowingly. 'The rest is up to you.' He made the continental gesture of counting notes with his thumb and forefinger. 'The management declines to interfere in private financial transactions.' He laughed, showing his gold molars then, stepping back even further, cried, 'Now let the procession of love commence!'

Under other circumstances, Seagram would have found the 'procession of love' an absolute farce. This mix of street girls and, probably, suburban housewives wobbled back and forth on their too-high heels, thrusting out their breasts, wiggling their behinds when they turned in what they obviously thought was a provocative manner. At regular intervals they raised their numbers, careful not to hide their breasts. It was rather like some provincial beauty contest, only now the stake was higher. They weren't here to win some cheap silver-plated cup; they were parading like this in their naive amateurish fashion in order to sell their bodies to the highest bidder.

Then he saw her: number nine with her sign the wrong way round so that it read six. That was typical of Mavis: she always got things wrong. But this night, wrong number or not, her cheap little prettyish face was set in a determined look. She was definitely here for the money and she was going to get it.

'Christ Almighty!' he yelled above the racket the excited officers were making.

'Mavis! What in God's name are you doing here?'

'Sit down!' they yelled. 'Let the cat have a look at the frigging canary!' And others cried, 'What the hell do you think she's doing here, shipmate – trying to raise money for the war effort?' To which a lone voice added plaintively, 'Well she's certainly raising something o' mine, chaps!'

For a moment Seagram didn't know whether to weep or scream. Mavis had always gone to extremes, but what a fool she was making of herself, and of him, too. He sprang to his feet, nearly upsetting the drunken lieutenant-commander's whisky. 'I say,' he said thickly. 'No use going on at it like that, old bean. It's only sex, you know!' Opposite him the ex-lower-decker burst into a mocking rendition of the old ditty, with 'And the mate at the wheel had a bloody good feel at the girl I left behind me...'

But Seagram was no longer hearing or seeing the mocking, laughing, red-flushed drunken faces all around him in the crowded club. He was pushing to where Mavis had come to a stop, her sharp little face a mixture of anger and surprise. 'Mavis,' he hissed through gritted teeth, 'drop that sign and come with me – this instant!'

'No,' she snapped, her voice shaky but determined at the same time.

'I won't ask you twice,' he said, feeling a muscle at the side of his face begin to twitch out of control. At that moment he could have strangled her with his bare hands. 'Have you no shame, Mavis...? In front of all these drunken louts.'

'No. I haven't. I'm sick of waiting for you ... I want some fun now, while I'm young.'

'You call this fun?' he snapped bitterly, trying to prevent himself from shouting. He reached for the stupid sign and tried to wrest it from her hands. But with surprising strength she hung on to it.

'Leave me alone,' she cried, and already the tears were beginning to stream down her thin cheeks leaving wet lines down the white face powder.

'No, drop it,' he ordered.

'Leave me alone,' she pleaded again, her knuckles white as she held on to the stupid sign with all her remaining strength.

'Leave her alone,' the drunken mob echoed. 'You can see she doesn't want you.'

At his table the ex-lower-decker was now singing, 'Where was the driver when the boiler bust? ... They found his bollocks and the same to you ... Bollocks...'

Seagram could take no more. He lunged at Mavis. He tried to grab the placard and pull it from her hands. In the last moment she twisted to one side. Instead of grabbing the sign, his hand caught and tore at her flimsy, cheap blouse. The cloth ripped easily. With it came the white cup of her bra revealing the small, pink-tipped breast below. Mavis screamed. She dropped the sign, and her hands flew to hide her breast from the crowd. They wolf-whistled until the drunken lieutenant commander rose unsteadily from his chair and cried to no one in particular, 'Arrest that man ... He's a sex fiend ... He has just attacked an innocent young woman—'

'Sit down, you drunken old fart,' the ex-lower-decker interrupted. 'You ought to be ruddy well ashamed o' yersen,' he snorted. He pulled at the other officer's tunic. The latter was caught off balance. He smashed into the table, upset the glasses with the tinkle of broken glass and slumped on the floor, snoring happily as soon as he hit it.

But now the damage was done. There were cries of sympathy for Mavis, who was standing there, hands in front of her pathetic little breast, all defiance vanished now, sobbing as if her heart was broken. '*Porco di Madonna*,' the swarthy waiter who had long pretended to be a Maltese shrieked in his native Italian. He rushed forward, waving his hands furiously, while the other girls milled around uncertain about what they should do, except for one of the professionals, who was doing some kind of clumsy awkward striptease as if she might attract a paying client in this manner.

The waiter grabbed Seagram by the shoulder. 'You go now,' he ordered, his English suddenly broken again. 'First you give me ten pounds English for broken items.'

That did it. It was the last straw for Seagram. He turned. Without even looking properly at the water, he launched a punch at him. It caught him directly on the point of his big, jutting nose. He yelled. The next instant he was falling backwards, blood jetting in a thick bright-red stream from his injured nostrils.

'Give it to 'em, Navy!' a Yank cried. 'Up the rebels!'

'Fuck the rebels!' an Irish voice called, and then it started. Bottles began to fly as did fists. In a flash all was chaos: men of half a dozen Allied forces punching each other for no apparent reason, waiters threatening to call the police and attempting to rescue as many bottles as they could, women scream-ing and huddling together for protection.

Seagram knew quite clearly, despite his rage, that he was ruining his career, for what it was worth, by getting involved in such a brawl. But somehow it didn't matter, for he could stand the shame of what Mavis had done to him no longer. With all his strength he punched her in the face – and afterwards he had to admit that he'd enjoyed it. She gave a sad little gasp. Her knees sagged like those of a new-born foal. He caught her before she fell. Next moment he was drag-ging her barely conscious body out of the club, oblivious to the fact that her naked breast was revealed for all to see, with the lower-decker officer singing behind him, in between taking gulps of the lieutenant-commander's drink, oblivious to the riot taking place around him. 'And the mate at the wheel had a bloody good feel at the girl I left behind me...'

Five

Lieutenant Seagram buckled on his sword, feeling a bit of a fool as he did so. All the same he did feel a sense of relief, too. He hadn't been cashiered after all, as Bert had predicted he might if he didn't play his cards right in front of the board of inquiry. 'You must remember, Charlie, that you're facing regular naval officers, who probably in their lengthy careers have buggered young blacks, fornicated with women of every colour and creed all over the world, and have been half-seas over for most of their career.' He gave his shipmate a weary, cynical smile. 'But they did those things overseas, out of the public eye. You, fool that you are, Charlie, justifiably, I must admit, have gone and duffed up your lawful in the public eye. Even got in the papers. Tut-tut ... bad news indeed, Charlie. But your DSC at Dunkirk might save you.'

It had. His DSC and the fact, as the president of the tribunal had put it, 'you have been subjected to extreme provocation, Lieutenant Seagram,' saved him from being cashiered or reduced to the ranks. He could continue to serve His Majesty, but he knew that as far as the senior service was concerned he'd be stamped for ever as 'the officer who gave his missus a black eye in a public brawl'. God knows what that would mean for the rest of his wartime career.

He stepped outside, blinking in the yellow rays of autumn sunshine. On the square a group of recruits were marching up and down, some of them out of step or unable to swing their arms correctly, being chivvied by a little terrier of an old chief petty officer, crying at them in a high falsetto, 'Come on, you pregnant penguins, swing them arms ... Bags o' swank now ... and open them legs ... If anything drops out, dear old CPO Rawlings'll pick it up fer yer!'

For a moment Seagram wished he were in the place of those recruits, however hard they might feel they were being treated. It would be a new start. He would not make the mistakes he had done in these more recent wartime years. But fate had decreed that this was what he was going to be: a discredited young lieutenant, whose career had come to an abrupt stop, with an ex-wife who was now living openly in sin with a fat American staff colonel who could have been her father. Seagram pulled a face in the same instant that a smart young signaller swung off his sit-up-and-beg official cycle and called, 'Lieutenant Seagram?'

'Yes,' he replied, though Seagram knew there was no real need to identify himself, for everyone in the Portsmouth barracks knew him as the bloke who beat up his missus when he found she was on the game, flogging it to the Yanks – at a price. After all, it had been reported in the *News of the World* the previous Sunday with Mavis being pictured quoted as saying she had found happiness at last. 'What is it?'

'You're wanted urgently at the office, sir. There's a Lieutenant Commander Challenger on the blower – er – phone, sir, from Scotland,' he added, as if it were important. 'If you like, sir, you can borrow my bicycle.'

It was Bert, and even over the line from the Clyde Seagram could sense the commander's excitement, as he boomed (Bert had never seemed really to get the hang of telephones), 'Congratulations, old fruit. I've already heard. Secret sources in Portsmouth and the Admiralty, you know, Charlie. You're cleared.'

Seagram looked around the office and the Wren typist looked away discreetly; obviously she, too, knew about him and his case. 'It was nip-and-tuck for a while. I thought that bloody admiral with a monocle was about to scupper me after the clerk read Mavis's testimony.'

'But he didn't, Charlie,' Challenger cried, 'and don't talk about bloody admirals like that, old bean. I hope to be a bloody admiral myself one day. Now I have to cut this short. There is a pretty first officer in the Wrens breathing down my neck. Good news, Charlie. You're coming back to the Patrol Service and we've been given a great job, which I can't tell you about over the blower, natch. Though I can tell you this: by the time you're back up here in this Scottish wilderness, I'll be gone.'

'Gone?'

'Yes. I've got a posting.' There was no mistaking the excitement in Challenger's voice. 'I'm to be given my first real command. A cruiser no less, even if she's only a light one. The new Dido class.'

'Congratulations, Bert. I'm very pleased for you.'

'And I'm very pleased for me, Charlie, you can imagine.' Challenger's voice grew serious. 'Now do me a favour, Charlie. I don't have to tell you that your name is mud in certain stuffy, old-fashioned quarters. No names, no pack drill. So they'll be out to get you if they can – clear?'

'Clear.'

At her desk the Wren waiting for him to finish had swung her long black-clad legs from beneath it and had opened them too carelessly. He could see the stretch of white flesh above the stocking tops – and she was smiling encouragingly.

Seagram frowned at her severely. He wasn't getting into that kind of business, not after Mavis's treachery. The Wren snapped her legs closed and tugged at her skirt as if he had just made an improper suggestion to her.

'So, Charlie,' Challenger was saying, 'promise me you'll keep your nose clean, and don't give the four-ringed buggers a chance to shop you. Above all, leave off the bottle, which has ruined so many officers up here in the Scottish wilderness – demon drink and all that. I know you've got a good reason to go on the booze after what happened. But *don't*.' The phone went dead and it would be two long years of war before he would see Challenger again.

69

For a while Seagram tried – and tried hard. The same old drunken skipper was in charge, and instead of criticizing him as he had done before, Seagram had taken over more of his responsibilities, especially when the gripper was suffering one of his 'ulcer attacks', confining him to his cabin.

He attempted to knock the hostilities-only men and handful of old hands into some sort of shape, giving them more than enough tasks when they were in port, trying to turn the rusty old tub of a ship into something akin to one of His Majesty's Royal Navy vessels. Instead of letting them lounge on the lower deck over their mops and brooms, leaning on the rail, smoking their Woods and passing the hours in complaint and idle chatter, he set them to work. He had them scaling, painting, even polishing the brasswork, 'as if this was the peacetime China frigging station,' he heard one old three-stripey complain. Behind his back the HO men started to call him 'fuckin' Cap'n Bligh', and even the old sot of a skipper advised him, 'Don't work 'em too hard, Charles. They aren't used to it. We don't want trouble, do we? Live and let live, I say.' When Seagram had tried to protest, the old skipper shuffled off to his cabin with yet another bottle of pink gin from the ward-room and was seen no more that day.

In those weeks immediately after his tribunal, Seagram certainly did try very hard to get his life straightened out once more. He was attentive to his duties, reading far into the night when they were in port, learning ever more about his profession in case he should ever be promoted. He stopped drinking almost totally, save for one single pink gin before dinner in the tiny wardroom he shared mostly with a clean shaven 'snotty' who didn't drink at all (the two of them rarely saw the skipper. He took his 'meals' – here the wardroom mess steward would often wink, indicating the skipper's dinner this night was to be a bottle of booze). Sometimes he went ashore, but never to the pubs like the rest. He usually went to the pictures, and when a young woman moved next to him, as they often did when they spotted an officer's uniform, he would find another seat. As he told himself, 'Charlie, old boy, no entanglements now. No booze, no women, just the work. All that sort of stuff is in the past.'

Unfortunately, as Charles Seagram was to find out, the past had a habit of catching up with you. For Seagram it came in the form of a long letter from Mavis. It was written in pencil, as if he were not worthy of ink, and he could see at first glance how she had broken off the pencil lead at several points. It was indicative of just how angry she had been when she had written the letter.

It was headed simply, 'To whom it may concern', and informed him right from the start in the very first line that Mavis was taking 'divorce proceedings' against him 'on the grounds of mental and physical cruelty'. He could understand the latter; after all, he had punched her hard in the Kit Kat. The 'mental' part was a mystery to him. But Mavis's bad temper had apparently got the better of her, and in the latter part of the letter she really let loose, accusing him of neglecting her while he pursued his naval career, thinking more of 'your toy boats than you did of me, all by myself in London ... Sometimes I thought you didn't want to come on leave to me in the first place. But then what did it matter, *you were never any good in bed anyway. You never satisfied me.*' Not only were the accusations underlined, but they were accompanied by at least half a dozen exclamation marks, as if she couldn't make her point clearly enough. She ended with 'My Joe' – she meant the American staff officer – 'might be a lot older than you, but he knows how to keep a woman happy – *in all ways.*' Again, the three words were underlined, as if she had taken pleasure in turning the knife in the wound and spelling out exactly what she thought of him in bed. It seemed to confirm what he'd suspected all along: that she'd always intended for him to catch her out and give her a reason to leave him. He couldn't think why else she would have left him with a note that night directing him to the Kit Kat

That night he got drunk with the skipper. Somehow he had got off the boat – how he would never know – and found one of the amateur whores who frequented the dock area. He had a vague memory of an older woman who smelled of spirits and sweat and who, after he had given her his last two pounds, had been kind to him in her rough-and-ready whore's fashion.

She had tried to excite him for a long time. She had played with him, stuck her tongue wetly in his ear, had put his hand under her blouse and let him feel her dangling heavy breasts until she had yelped with pain when he had pressed her big nipples too hard. She had even promised to give him the supreme pleasure – 'the gamarrouche' as she called it

73

– if he'd give her an extra five shillings. She hadn't minded when he had said he hadn't five bob left, and had undone his flies and done it all the same. But it hadn't worked; nothing had worked, so he had been close to tears of self-pity and frustration when she had given up on him, giving him a pat on the shoulder like a fond mother might to a child, saying, 'Dinna fash yersen, sonny, it'll no be the last time ... happens to all you fine buckos o' young men.'

She had been right. It had happened again, and in the end he simply gave up. Mavis had been right. She had won. Now, this summer of 1942, the bottle seemed the only solace and, although he could not allow himself as 'number one' to get into the same state as the skipper with his 'ulcers', he usually took to his cabin after dinner when they were in port and drank himself into insensibility in the privacy of his dirty little cabin, the frames which once enclosed the pictures of Mavis and himself on their marriage day and their brief honeymoon at Brighton staring back at him empty, like blinded eyes.

Seagram was no fool. He knew quite clearly, even in those drink-sodden evenings in the loneliness of his little cabin with the waves lapping across the hull, that he was wallowing in self-pity and that it was ruining not only his naval career, but his whole life. At such times he told himself that he needed real action, not these damned boring routine patrols. Since Challenger had promised him excitement in the form of action during that last telephone call before he had been posted to his new command, nothing really out of the ordinary had happened. Now, he promised himself, once the real call to action came, he'd kick the drinking habit and become his old self.

But when the call did come Charles Seagram failed to answer it in the manner he'd thought he would...

It was a lovely clear autumn morning. The sun was bright, but it was still bitterly cold, with the wind coming, it seemed, straight from the Arctic. They had just had the usual Sunday morning rounds, with the little ships still sailing line abreast, when the order came to spend an hour practising the radar control of the three-inch guns that most of the ships carried. On the bridges of the ships the leading hands would then be kept busy painting the arcs of fire for each gun on the gyro-repeater compass.

It was all very routine, but the night before

75

Seagram had gone ashore and had bumped into the skipper, already well-oiled, as he called it, who hadn't taken long to persuade his number one to go on a pub crawl. Despite the knowledge that they would be sailing at dawn, Seagram had gone along with the suggestion. Thus it was that this morning he had a splitting headache, a bad tremble in his hands and was in a foul temper. He had protested at the state of the mess deck and the heads, although they were in their usual state of dirt and disorder. Then he discovered they had run out of the grey-green paint they used for painting the figures on the gyro-repeater compass, just before he and the skipper were scheduled to go to the wardroom for a pre-luncheon drink – and he was dying for a cold beer to quench his raging thirst and perhaps another hair of the dog, which might soothe his hangover.

Naturally he blew his top, shouting at the earnest storeman, one of the few on the lower deck who took his duties seriously. 'Christ Almighty, what have you got in that bloody head of yours, Jenkins, – bloody porridge? Can't you ever get—' He never finished his outburst, for in that very same instant there was the well-known hollow

76

boom of metal striking metal to starboard, followed an instant later by an angry spurt of cherry-red flame. 'Someone's stopped one, sir,' Jenkins cried, and as Seagram's head turned in the direction of the explosion he could see something turning over in the water like a gigantic metal whale spouting flame instead of water all the while. 'In God's name,' he yelled above the roar of the flames which seared the length of the dying ship like a gigantic blowtorch, 'they've got *Tug o'War*.'

'You bet they have, sir,' Jenkins gasped in horror as a severed arm flew through the air and landed on the deck below with a plop, spraying bright-red blood in a dozen different directions.

But Seagram, head aching, all thoughts of that cold beer vanished now, had no time to ponder the fate of the first of the flotilla to be hit. As they sailed on, past where the *Tug o'War* was going down, water pouring down its old-fashioned funnel making a gurgling sound like an enormous bath drain, the signals started to flash back and forth, the 'sparks' and 'bunts' running up to the bridges with their urgent messages, all of which made the one overwhelming point: one of the *Queens* was approaching fast and there were U-boats about. If something wasn't done soon, with the unarmed, un-accompanied eighty-thousand-ton pride of the British Merchant Navy closing on them at thirty knots, a tragedy was in the making.

Six

'We're poor little lambs who have lost our way,' they sang, as they lined up for chow. 'Baa ... baa.' Not that many of them wanted the food served by the English cooks of the *Queen Mary*. Brussels sprouts, mashed potatoes and stewed kidneys weren't their idea of food. But those of the ten thousand US servicemen on board the great liner who had now overcome their sea sickness were hungry, especially as the wind was freshening and the air was becoming cooler as they came ever closer to Liverpool, giving them an appetite. Five days without food for most of them and, as one of them wisecracked, 'Guys, I could even eat shit on shingle again.' The stewed poor quality beef on toast had made up much of their army rations. So the lines snaked right across the great ship, back and forth, twenty-four hours a day, with the filthy cooks in their greasy overalls, sweating into their cauldrons as they dished out great dripping ladles of the nauseating mess.

But while the Yanks lined up and moaned and hundreds of others lay on the tiered bunks below, green-faced and wretched with sickness, the British and American army officers on the bridge worried, for by now they were aware of the U-boat packs lurking in the Irish Sea like predatory wolves, using the neutral waters to prepare their attack on the pride of the British merchant fleet, the *Queen Mary*.

The captain, big and bluff, did not show his fears, but already he was taking appropriate measures. He had informed the crew what was happening, but not their GI passengers; he didn't want any panic. But the black flag signifying an alert had been raised, and double lookouts were posted.

Now the commander of the *Queen Mary* ordered the bridge to zigzag more frequently to put any lurking U-boat skipper off his aim. At thirty knots the great ship changed course every quarter of a sea mile, placing a tremendous strain on the helmsman, whose face dripped with sweat with the effort. In the meantime he signalled the flag captain at Liverpool for every available assistance – just in case. As he confided in his first officer in an urgent whispered conversation out of earshot of the others on the bridge, 'We've got some two thousand soldiers for whom we've got no life-saving facilities ... Better have the men ready to break up the deck if necessary.' The first officer had looked at the captain, shocked. The *Queen*'s deck was almost holy. Even in wartime, when they had a chance, the crew sandstoned it a bright white. Now they were perhaps to chop it up.

Half an hour later the tension eased somewhat when a Coastal Command Sunderland appeared off the great ship's portside. Naturally those Yanks who were on deck cried, 'Say, guys, look at that. One of our planes so far out to sea.'

British members of the crew standing nearby laughed sardonically. It was typical. The Yanks thought that anything that looked big or modern had to be American. On the very first day when they had sailed from New York, the story had done the rounds of the ship's crew of the Yank who had smirked and exclaimed, 'How come you Britishers

80

can't build a ship like this in your country?' Some time later the 'Britishers' had had their revenge when the Red Ensign of the British Merchant Service had been hoisted and the Americans who weren't already seasick had realized that this was a ship built by 'Britishers'.

Now the white-painted flying boat circled the great ship slowly, as its signaller started to flash his aldis lamp off and on smartly. Below, 'flags', as the ships' signallers were named, stood on the edge of the bridge taking down the signal, while the Yanks wondered what was going on. Minutes later they found out, as the senior American officer on board the *Queen* spoke to them over the booming echoing tannoy address system. 'Now hear this ... now hear this! We are some fifty miles away from the British port of Liverpool where we'll dock before nightfall.' That announcement was greeted with weak cheers from the GIs, who had suffered so much sickness on the trip from New York. A voice called, 'Perhaps we'll get some good hometown style American chow then, instead of this limey—'

'Knock it off, soldier,' a top sergeant interrupted. 'Let's listen, big mouth.'

Just in time they heard the senior officer

81

say, 'We had been expecting some trouble from enemy underwater craft. But the captain says we've just had good news from that flying boat. A British group, including a cruiser, is coming out to meet us. The rendezvous is planned for approximately thirteen hundred hours – that's one o'clock this afternoon to some of you dopes. I think, men, our troubles are over. Over and out.' The tannoy address system went dead and a few of the GIs cheered – but not many – as if some sort of victory had been won.

All the same, more and more GIs, now wearing their lifebelts as ordered, started to cram the rails despite the stiff breeze, peering towards the west from which direction the relief force would come, hoping to catch a first glimpse of the British ships and then the land beyond. Even the poker games, which had been going for four days, ever since they had sailed from the New York piers, were abandoned. Now the GIs were concerned one hundred per cent with getting their feet on the good solid ground, even if it were British.

Even the *Queen*'s captain felt a sense of relief. He ordered, 'Lower the black flag, I think we can call the alert off.'

'And the speed, sir?' his chief officer asked.

The captain flung a glance to their front. The sea was clear and he estimated the visibility was still about half a mile. That would give him enough time and space to alter course if another ship appeared. He ordered, 'Stop the zigzag, please. But keep up the speed. Thirty knots.'

For a moment it seemed to the others on the bridge that afternoon that the chief officer might object, and they knew why: coastal fog came in quickly in these waters and soon they'd be meeting myriad small craft as well as the cruiser come to protect them from any lurking German U-boat. The chance of a collision in those circumstances was very real. But when the chief officer answered, he raised no objection. 'Ay, ay, sir,' he said, 'thirty knots it is, sir.'

So the great ship sailed on...

Charlie Seagram was angry still. Indeed, he was angrier than ever. As soon as they had left port, the skipper had put on his old act. He had held his stomach, rolled his eyes, moaned, gasped and then said in a theatrically weak voice, 'Charlie, old lad, you'd better take over. My guts are hurting like hell ... the bloody ulcers are acting up a-soddin'-gain. Just go to the wardroom and see if I can get a cup of tea and then I'll go to my cabin for a lie-down.'

Even before Seagram had been able to protest, the skipper had staggered off to the tiny wardroom to get his 'cup of tea', which came in the form of a bottle labelled pink gin or rum, leaving Seagram, who didn't feel particularly well himself, on his own. If that hadn't been enough, the old tub had started losing speed, and the flotilla commander had rounded on him through the loud hailer, yelling angrily across the sea, now filled with the dead and dying of the *Tug O' War*, 'Can't you bloody well keep station? You've just seen what happened. Do you want a bloody tin kipper' – a torpedo – 'up your bloody slow arse too?'

Charlie Seagram certainly didn't. One of the flotilla had been ordered to stop and rescue the survivors of the torpedoed vessel, and they didn't look good: half a dozen shivering men, their faces black and gleaming with oil, dazed and bewildered, looking as if they couldn't believe this was happening. But they weren't the worst of it. It was the choking cries of the men who were drowning before they could be rescued, whimpering in their death throes, crying for 'mates' who would never come and 'mothers' they'd never see again.

In the end, Seagram just turned his head away, concentrating on his duties until they were through; until there were no more cries for help and no struggling shadows in the wreckage and the dead were alone, floating face upwards like so many dead fish in that black heaving waste. Then he went into the wardroom, picked up the bottle of pink gin from the pantry and took a hefty drink straight from the bottle, and then, as if as an afterthought, another one. When he returned on deck, he was already half drunk, his senses numbed, for a while at peace with this terrible world of misery and sudden death...

An hour passed. The flotilla was spread out in a rough line abreast, asdic operators, ears glued to their machines, trying to pick up the signals of the U-boats still probably lurking under the surface of the sea. Everywhere, the skippers of the little craft had doubled their forward lookouts, trying to catch any submarine on the surface but also their first sight of the *Queen*. At regular intervals, lone Beaufighters swept down, churning up the sea with their propwash, attempting to do the same thing. Everything seemed under control and even Seagram, as foul tempered as he had been, started to relax. He knew he could handle the situation now, even with the drunken skipper on his hands and the reluctant, ill-disciplined 'heroes' who made up his crew.

Thus it was, just as the light cruiser which would add muscle to the force of little ships hove into sight, that he decided his presence on the bridge wouldn't be missed for ten minutes; he'd go and enjoy what he called his 'mid-afternoon refreshment', and he was not thinking of tea. Ordering the helmsmen to stick to the flotilla course and telling the gnarled old petty officer with the ribbons of the Old War to keep him informed immediately if anything transpired, he finished with, 'Going below to see how the captain's getting on. He might be in pain and need a tablet or something.'

'Ay ay, sir,' the old chiefie answered smartly. But as he disappeared below, the chiefie raised his fingers to his mouth as if he were lifting a glass, sneering, 'Tablet my arse! More likely a mug o' grog.' He shook his grizzled head, as if he couldn't comprehend the world any more. 'Officers and gents these days – Christ on a crutch – *I've shat 'em!*'

* * *

The fog came in quite unexpectedly. One moment the afternoon was relatively clear, the next the fog from the land was creeping in like a silent-footed grey cat. Up on the bridge of the *Queen* they weren't overly worried, though the captain was summoned up from his day cabin to take charge. Privately he thought his senior officer was being too fussy and careful. Still, he'd been a young officer at the time of the sinking of the *Titanic* and that drastic lesson had never left him. As he lectured his own junior officers, 'Better be safe than sorry.' So he came up to the bridge, still adjusting his tie, for he had been taking a cat nap as he usually did at this time of the day, thanked the senior officer, checked with the radar officer, warned the visual lookouts to be on their toes and then stared out at the thickening wall of fog.

At two thirty he was informed that the *Queen* was closing fast with the flotilla coming out to escort them into Liverpool. Again he did his checks and issued his warnings. At the same time he contacted the flag officer at Liverpool and asked for instructions about his speed; the great ship was still travelling at thirty knots. He was told to maintain that speed until he linked up with the navy and, in particular, with the light cruiser, *HMS Curacoa*. According to the flag officer on shore, he was dead on course, sailing at a speed of some twenty-five knots, the maximum her boilers could produce. The *Queen*'s captain pointed out that he was experiencing some fog and that visibility was down to approximately a quarter of a mile. At the speed the two ships were approaching each other and with poor visibility, maintaining his current speed could be dangerous. The flag officer in Liverpool disagreed. Besides he signalled, 'You know who is watching this one, if you know who I mean.'

The captain did. Churchill. The Grand Old Man took a personal interest, he knew, in each voyage of the *Queens* bringing American troops across the Atlantic. It was as if the success of the war depended on just how many were transported each time. He concluded that perhaps Churchill was right. At all events he was going to be the last man to incur the Prime Minister's displeasure. He relayed the flag officer message to his senior officer and added, when he saw the anxious look on the latter's face, 'Don't worry, old chap. Mr Churchill is up there in the clouds personally watching over us like a guardian angel.'

The senior officer didn't seem very reassured by the news. Outside the fog thickened.

Charlie Seagram decided he could afford another one. The wardroom steward was down below preparing dinner and he was alone in the tiny cabin with its dogeared copies of the *Illustrated London News* and its battered, split leather furniture. 'I think I could afford another snifter,' he said aloud. It was customary that he should have summoned the wardroom steward to fix him a drink, but he didn't want the little nancy boy with his mincing manner, who was a great gossip, to learn just how much he was drinking these days. Otherwise it would have been all over the ship. Instead he reached for his special bottle of pink gin which he routinely filled with water when it got below his 'mark', and poured himself his 'snifter'; he would fill it up to the correct level afterwards. At the moment he was too greedy for the burn of the strong gin to worry about such matters. Still, he made himself take his time. He didn't want to be like the skipper, who didn't seem to care how greedily other officers saw him swallow the booze in the wardoom. So he raised the glass, watching his hand tremble badly as he did so, and faced the portrait of the poor stuttering King-Emperor George VI. 'A toast to Your Majesty,' he proclaimed and, steadying his hand the best he could, brought the glass to his lips. But he wasn't fated to swallow the pink gin this day.

Suddenly, startlingly, the whole craft shuddered violently. He was blinded by a flash of brilliant scarlet flame through the porthole. The glass dropped and shattered to a thousand pieces on the wardroom floor as the deck rose and fell alarmingly. He held on to the wardroom table as if his very life depended upon it, as the hull of the vessel was peppered by what seemed to be shrapnel. Again the craft heaved violently, and then the cynical little petty officer was crying down the voicetube, 'Get up on deck right away, sir.'

'What—'

The petty officer cut him off, with almost a note of hysteria in his voice. 'For God's sake, sir, right away. Something terrible's happened ... Oh my God—' he broke off as if he were so overcome by emotion that he could no longer speak.

For a moment, Seagram was too surprised to know what to do. Fortunately the bottle of pink gin was still intact. Instinctively he took a hefty swig at it, coughed thickly and then, grabbing his battered, tarnished cap, pushed his way through the door and the crowd of excited sailors who had deserted their posts in their usual ill-disciplined fashion and were gawping and pointing to the west, where the sky had turned a vivid scarlet hue.

'Get back to your stations!' he began angrily, and then stopped short as suddenly he caught a glimpse of what they were staring at. To their immediate front, the light cruiser had come to an abrupt stop. Flames were shooting out from her shattered bow. To her port the huge liner, which had to be the *Queen Mary*, the ship they had come to escort to Liverpool, was slowing down, but not dramatically. For a moment Seagram thought that the cruiser had been torpedoed. But then he saw that she wasn't flying the black alert flag, which would indicate that there was an enemy in the general area. Abruptly it dawned upon him, as he saw that the huge bow of the *Queen* was crumpled and holed above the waterline. 'Oh my God,' he commenced, but the ashen-faced CPO from the bridge beat him to it, 'The *Queen* hit her, sir ... There's been a collision, sir ... Better get up to the bridge ... The flotilla leader is on the blower.'

For a moment Seagram was rooted to the spot. He couldn't seem to move. The tragedy he was witnessing was too great. The *Queen* had collided with one of their own ships, and he could see already she was moving off, although men of the cruiser's crew were jumping into the water on all sides, as she started to sink rapidly.

'*Sir*!' The petty officer's urgent appeal cut into his awe stricken reverie. 'The flotilla leader, sir.'

Seagram shook his head hard like a man attempting to wake from a heavy, drugged sleep. He heard himself say, 'I'm coming ... Go and wake the skipper. At the double, for Chrissake.'

'Ay ay, sir.' The CPO doubled away with more alacrity than Seagram had ever seen him display. The shock of the tragedy was obviously having an effect, even on him.

Seagram pushed his way through the sailors and clambered up to the bridge. He clicked on the apparatus.

'What in God's name took you so long?' The flotilla leader's voice came through, hard and incisive, though even he couldn't quite control his shock.

'Sorry, sir,' Seagram answered, putting every effort he had into controlling his own voice.

'Where's your skipper?' the flotilla leader demanded in a hurry.

'Not too well—'

'Oh he's at the bottle again, eh,' the other man broke in harshly. 'All right, Seagram, you're in charge. The *Queen Mary* has been ordered to continue at top speed. Yes, I know, but that's the way it is. The *Queen* and her Yanks are more important than our own poor lads out there drowning at this very moment. So this is what you do.' Hurriedly he gave the still tipsy young officer his instructions as the skipper came staggering into the bridgehouse, holding a hand to his head and moaning softly. He ended with, 'There'll be only the two of you. The rest of the flotilla has been ordered to escort the *Queen* into Liverpool ... I know, I know,' he said testily, as if Seagram were about to object. 'But they say the order has come from Winnie, and who am I to argue with *him*.' The flotilla leader drew a deep breath, as if he were already at the end of his tether. 'All right, Seagram, you're on your own. Don't let that old sot of a skipper get in your way. But above everything else, Seagram,

save as many of our lads as you can, *please*.'
There was a sudden note of despair in his
voice. 'They deserve better from the Royal
Navy and the country than to die at the
hands of their own countrymen. Over and
out.'

The phone went dead. Next to him the
skipper moaned yet again and sighed,
'Christ, could I just do with a drink...'

Seven

Seagram, appalled by what had happened,
had no time for the skipper, whose only
concern seemed to be to have another drink.
The pitiful cries for help coming from
outside didn't move the older man. Drink
was what he wanted; nothing more. In a fit
of anger, knowing that, sot though the
skipper was, he was talking to his superior
officer, Seagram lashed out with, 'Oh fuck
off to your cabin and drink yourself more
stupid than you are. I can't use you here.'

Surprisingly enough the skipper did exactly that, and the astonished little CPO

said, 'Well, I'll stone the crows, sir! Never thought anyone would tell the old man off like that.'

Seagram ignored the comment. He had work to do – and he needed to move fast because it was already beginning to grow dark and there were pitiful survivors of the collision everywhere in darkening waters. 'All right, helmsmen,' he ordered, 'slow ahead. Petty Officer, come with me.'

As the craft slowed down to a snail's pace, the engines ticking over just sufficiently for the boat not to be swept off course by the mounting swell, the two of them surveyed the scene. All around them, the crew, normally so slovenly and rebellious, had armed themselves with poles, boathooks, even chairs – anything to which a drowning sailor could cling until he was hauled aboard.

Seagram was appalled by what he saw. It was a scene of absolute horror. So many of the matelots seemed so helpless. There was just one long continuous moan over the water, as the men crowded instinctively together, praying and calling for help. 'Help me ... help me, shipmate,' they moaned over and over again. Some pleaded, 'I've got a wife and kids back home at Pompey,' as if that might make them different from the rest, who were calling for their mothers or shouting the Lord's Prayer at the top of their voices. Here and there those who were going under for the last time grabbed at their shipmates and, crying hysterically, 'Don't let me go', clung on to them, dragging them down too.

Wild frantic fights broke out as those who were still afloat fought off the killing clutches of those going under. 'Get your fucking hands off me!' they cried and spluttered. 'Look after yoursen, you bastard! Do yer want to drown me as well?' Even above the screams, a horrified Seagram could hear the hard slap of hands or fists as they fought each other, as bitterly as they would have done any enemy.

Seagram now set about the task of rescuing as many of the sailors from the sinking cruiser as he could on the port side, while the other ship disappeared to starboard. The crew helped willingly enough, at first. Many of the men wore lifebelts, but they weren't working properly. Men kept going under, appearing spluttering and spewing water and then disappearing beneath the surface of the sea once more. It was hard to say whether they were dead or not, for the lifebelts held the dead only inches below the surface. Even with them it was necessary for the survivors, and there were hundreds of them, to keep moving arms and legs. But the men grew steadily more exhausted in their efforts to keep their heads above water. Others were already beginning to drift away, screaming with fear as they were carried into the growing darkness by the current. And all the time the light cruiser, split now into two sections, was getting ever lower in the water.

Seagram made a snap decision. As the craft moved at a snail's pace through the men bobbing up and down on the swell and his crew rescued those who were still alive, overcoming their horror at the task, pushing back those who were dead, held close to the surface by their lifebelts, he headed for the stern of the cruiser. Her screws were already high out of the water, as she prepared for her final plunge. In the fading light he could see the men packed high on the towering stern, crying and waving their arms.

Seagram could guess their dilemma. They knew the rump was ready to plunge beneath the sea and would take them with her to a watery grave. But they were afraid to jump. The distance to the sea was too far, and at the same time, even if they did dive over the side, would they escape being dragged down by the ship when she slid under? It was, he reasoned, his task to make those men jump and then rescue them as speedily as he could. He bit his bottom lip and frowned hard. How was he going to save them and at the same time avoid swamping those of the survivors already in the water who were still alive? It was a difficult decision that it seemed to be taking his drink-addled brain a long time to reach. But he knew he had to – and bloody soon. Men were dying on all sides and soon they'd be more if he didn't act. Besides, it was getting rapidly darker. He made his decision.

'Chiefie,' he yelled up to the bridge where the little CPO was positioned next to the helmsman, the latter's face streaming with sweat as he attempted to steer a course through the men in the water, knowing that if he caught them in the ship's screws they would be horribly mangled to death.

'Sir?'

'We're going to drop a boat. Get a leading hand ... Tell him to pick a handful of decent men and head for the *Curacoa*'s stern.'

'Ay ay, sir,' the CPO answered smartly, though at any other time he would have laughed out loud at that 'decent men'. 'I'll get Jenkins, sir.'

'Good. Tell him to keep well clear of the rump. I don't want any more casualties. But he's got to encourage the poor bastards to jump. Then he can lead them back to us. It's not the best of solutions, but it's the only one I can think of.'

'Sir,' the little chiefie snapped and then set off to find Jenkins and a crew at the double.

Seagram forgot about the boat immediately. Gagging at the stench of diesel oil rising from the sea and trying not to hear the pitiful cries of the survivors all around, he concentrated on getting as many of them on board as possible before the light failed altogether.

Seagram was horrified at their appearance. They came in batches, hardly able to haul themselves over the side. They were all dripping oil, black-faced and shivering with shock; here and there were the blood-red patches in the black covering of oil where they had been wounded. One had what appeared at first sight to be a perfectly clean pink arm. But on closer inspection, a shocked Seagram saw that his right arm had been flayed by steam of all its upper flesh, right to the elbow. Below, his bones gleamed like polished white ivory. He turned away sickened.

Now and again one of the rescuers would say in a matter of-fact manner, 'No use bothering with him, shipmate – he's snuffed it already,' and someone else would join in in the same callous way, with, 'Give him a push with yer grapnel ... He's a stiff. No room for stiffs on board.'

Once Seagram looked over the side at one of these 'stiffs', floating on his back in the water, his hair grey, face hollow, for he had forgotten his false teeth in his haste to escape. He didn't look one bit like a sailor on active service should. To Seagram he appeared more like an old grandad who should be sitting in front of a coal fire on a cold evening like this, smoking his clay pipe reflectively and listening to the radio. Instead he was dead, abandoned to the sea, never to be reunited with his family. At that moment Seagram was stone-cold sober, knowing somehow or other with the instancy of a vision that sooner or later they were all going to die alone and be abandoned to the grey-green unfeeling sea.

The sudden lurch beneath his feet that made him grab for the nearest stanchion shocked him out of his momentary reverie. 'What the hell?' he began, but already, before he could finish his question, the little craft's engines coughed, faltered, started again and then stopped altogether. Suddenly the ship was bobbing up and down on the surface of the water without power. Ahead the stern of the cruiser was beginning its death plunge, and, outlined dramatically by the setting sun, stark black against the blood-red ball of light, men, screaming as they did so, started to dive into the abruptly boiling sea.

Seagram bit his bottom lip impotently. He knew without asking what had happened. The months, perhaps years, of neglect under the vessel's drunken skipper had had their effect at last. The boilers, not properly maintained and cleaned out at regular intervals, as they should have been, had packed up; and even if they did manage to get the engines working again, he knew it would be too late to rescue the last survivors of the cruiser. He – for he knew in his heart of hearts that it was his fault – should have done something even if the drunk in charge was supposed to be the final authority. He had failed again. Slowly, trying to ignore the cries for help and the yells of pain all around him, he walked back the wardroom for the rest of the pink gin. There was nothing more he could do. The crew would attend to the sick. He was finished this time...

BOOK TWO

The Secret Invaders

The day shall come, the great avenging day.

Alexander Pope

One

The men were sprawled out on the cropped grass. Their collars were open, their faces were red with effort, and most of them were puffing at the Woodbines or drinking tea from their awkward square mess tins. A few of the hardier ones managed to munch iron-hard rock buns, with few precious currants, handed out by the girls at the 'Sally Ann' canteen opposite. Here and there a soldier lay face down on the grass, rifle thrown carelessly on one side, too worn out by the morning's exercise to even smoke.

'You work 'em hard, Colonel,' Seagram said to Colonel Ferguson, who seemed as fresh as ever although he had taken part in the same strenuous exercise.

Ferguson nodded. 'They're used to it. All of 'em were with me in Sicily and then at Salerno. They're used to hard work. All engineers are.' He looked directly at Seagram, who was now clad in navy-blue

105

battledress instead of the usual Royal Navy tunic. 'You look as if you've been doing some hard work yourself since I last saw you. You've lost weight, and if you don't mind my saying so, Seagram, you've lost a lot of that belly of yours.'

Seagram smiled. It had been tough, but now he was down to half a pint of beer a day and a pint a day whenever he had a weekend off – and that wasn't often since he had become a 'bigot' and had been sent to train with such troops as Ferguson's Assault Engineer Squadron, who would attack the beaches on D-Day.

'Thank you, sir. It's been a tough month. The brown jobs' – he meant the army – 'have sweated me down to a shadow of my former self.'

Ferguson shared his smile. But he already knew that it wasn't only the hard physical exercise which had made Seagram lose weight and removed that pudgy unhealthy look from the naval officer's face. His spies had also reported that Seagram had cut down his drinking radically. It was something for which he was very grateful. In what was to come, he couldn't afford to have any weak links, for the success of the Iron Division's assault might well rest on the success of his own daring mission. When that took place, he wanted to be able to rely on Seagram totally.

'Gentlemen.' It was the brigade sergeant major.

Ferguson and Seagram swung round. Immaculate despite the recent exercise, pacing stick set rigidly beneath his right arm, the NCO towered above the two officers, gaze set on some distant object.

'Yes?' Ferguson enquired.

'Brigadier wants an "O" Group, sir. Five minutes briefing for the officers before the men are dismissed.'

Ferguson nodded. 'Will do.' He turned to Seagram after returning the sergeant major's tremendous salute. 'Well, come along, Seagram. You can attend too. You're one of us now.' He lowered his voice. 'An infamous bigot.' He smiled winningly.

It was a mild joke. Seagram knew that. Still, he was pleased. He had been accepted again. After all these years of disgrace, feeling very much a failure, an outcast, first Challenger and now this tough lean engineer colonel had taken him up and made him realize that he was still of some use, that there was still a future for him. He smiled back and then the two of them strode across the grass to where the brigadier of the Iron Division, seated on a shooting stick, waited for them on the edge of the cliff.

The brigadier smiled at him, his broad, ruddy face adorned by a typical bushy army moustache, and announced, 'Well, gentlemen, the last exercise.' He raised his silver hip flask as if in toast and drank whatever it contained, and for the first time in years Lieutenant Seagram wasn't envious. He coughed as the powerful spirits hit his gullet and added, 'The next time we go, gentlemen, it will be the real thing. Shot and shell, the whole thing.' Again he smiled.

The senior officers showed no particular sign of animation. They had been through it before; they knew what to expect. The younger ones were obviously thrilled. They gushed, 'Good show!' or 'At last!' or 'That's the stuff to give the troops!' Here and there older men shook hands solemnly. Junior ones slapped each other on the back, as if they had achieved something very important. Ferguson, face revealing not too much, told himself it had been a bloody long time. Once, after Dunkirk when the Boche had thrown the defeated, disgraced British Army out of Europe he had thought this moment would never arrive. Now it had. He hoped that this time would be the last time.

Over the four years since Dunkirk there had been defeat after defeat. The British soldier seemed to have lost the ability to fight. He had heard that Churchill had moaned, 'Will the buggers ever bloody well fight?' Well now they were going to have to. For four years they had trained. Indeed, Ferguson thought, training had become for most squaddies an end in itself. Now at last they were facing the real thing. They would leave behind their uneventful, almost peace-time existence, broken only by the occasional air raid. Now they would venture out across that dark-green, heaving sea beyond the white cliffs and meet the unknown realities of battle.

The brigadier's somewhat fruity voice broke into his reverie. 'It's about time we got the chaps back to their camps, gentlemen. I hear on the QT that the cook wallahs are preparing something special for them tonight, now we're finished with training. There's much talk of fried eggs – eggs from real chickens, not those that produce dried eggs, made in the US.'

The officers laughed politely at his sally. Junior officers always did when brigadiers cracked jokes, however weak. The brigadier beamed at them.

'The chaps deserve it,' he continued. 'They have done us proud. Soon they're going to be sealed in their cages. They should be spoilt.' His smile vanished. 'Not so many of them will be coming back from there.' And they all knew where 'there' was.

Behind them the NCOs were rounding up their men. They might snap, but they too knew that this was the end of one phase of their existence. A new, more realistic and deadlier one would soon commence. 'All right, get fell in ... come on you dozy buggers, move them legs ... There's NAAFI bangers and fried eggs for first-comers tonight in the cookhouse ... Them cookhouse wallahs won't be flogging yer rations this night ... Come on there – GIT ON PARADE!'

'Train hard, fight easy,' the brigadier commented as he folded his shooting stick, well pleased with himself, as the senior officers walked back to their waiting staff cars, leaving the junior officers to march the men back to the camp.

Seagram was about to follow suit, but Ferguson caught him swiftly and held him back. 'Just a few words in your shell-like, Seagram, before we go back to the mess.'

'Yes?'

Ferguson lowered his voice as a platoon of the assault infantry marched off, smartly swinging their arms and singing lustily, 'I've got sixpence, jolly-jolly sixpence. I've got twopence to spend, twopence to lend and twopence to send home to my wife. No cares have I to grieve me, no pretty little girls to deceive me...' The colonel smiled as they swung by him with the platoon sergeant crying, 'Eyes right!'

'If life were only that simple, Seagram. All right, *their* training might have finished, but yours has really just begun.'

'Carry on, Colonel,' Seagram responded curiously.

'As I go rolling home ... by the light of the silvery moon,' the infantry were singing as they disappeared over the brow of the hill, heading for those delightful promised fried eggs. 'Happy is the day when the soldier gets his pay ... rolling home ... rolling home...'

As in the distance the singing of the infantry died away, overpowered now by the crash of the waves against the base of the tall white cliff. Ferguson stared out thoughtfully at the dark smudge on the horizon that was France. At his side Seagram waited expectantly for the engineer colonel to tell him what form his own special training was going to take. But for a moment Ferguson seemed to have his mind on other things. He said, as though speaking to himself, 'Soon, Seagram, a quarter of a million men will be landing on that coast yonder, carried there by over five thousand ships. What Philip of Spain failed to do, what Napoleon tried and failed at and what Hitler has never had the conviction or courage to try, we are about to do – and with God's grace we shall succeed.' His words sent a shiver down Seagram's spine and for the first time he realized the enormity of the undertaking which he and all the rest, down to those hungry infantrymen marching away in the distance in the fading light, had been committed.

'Yet,' Ferguson went on, 'if one link in that huge chain is broken, the whole massive operation will collapse. For years now the planners have been attempting to solve every possible contingency, down even to the exact number of bullets each infantryman should carry. Now this damned bunker crops up – absolutely out of the bloody blue.' There was a note of exasperation in Ferguson's voice, as if the bunker went against his engineer's sense of order. 'Now I've had a look at it and there seems only one way to get at it and destroy the thing before it has a chance to ruin the whole D-Day op, which it could well do, believe you me.'

'And what did the photo reveal, sir?'

'*Photo!*' Ferguson turned on him. 'Who said anything about a photo, Seagram, eh?'

The younger officer looked at Ferguson totally confused. 'Well, I thought you said, sir, that you'd had a look at it...' His words stuttered and died away as Ferguson's exasperation turned to a gentle if somewhat mocking smile.

'I did. This last week, to be exact.' He nodded to where the coast of France had disappeared into the darkness. 'Over there.'

'You mean you were in *France*, sir?'

'Yes, I've been there a couple of times since the beginning of the year – totally hush-hush naturally. As a bigot, I'm not allowed to venture on to enemy territory before the balloon goes up. The Gestapo might do some nasty things to my fingernails and even worse to other parts of my manly torso in order to force the secret of D-Day out of my tightly sealed lips.'

Seagram looked at the colonel, totally amazed by this new revelation. 'You mean you parachuted into France, sir?'

'No, I don't. You wouldn't get me to jump out of an aeroplane attached to a bit of knicker silk for all the money in the mint.' His smile broadened. 'I went courtesy of the COPP. It will be the same secret organization that will take us *both* across before this week is out.'

'COPP.' Seagram repeated the word slowly. 'What does it stand for, sir?'

Ferguson smirked. 'The organization is so secret, Seagram, that I shouldn't even tell you what the initials stand for. But I will, seeing that it will be responsible for getting you and me safely to and back from France in a couple of days. You can swim, I suppose?' he added, and said, without waiting for an answer, 'The initials stand for "Combined Operations Pilotage Parties".' He saw the still-puzzled look on the naval officer's face and explained quickly, 'Don't mean much does it. I'm not surprised. Even the unit title is not supposed to reveal anything about the unit's activities. They are frankly very daring. Indeed I suspect that if the Hun ever got hold of any of the pilotage people, they'd shoot 'em in the end. Not a pleasant prospect.' He cleared his throat and looked keenly at Seagram, as if checking whether his words had frightened the other officer.

They hadn't. After what he had been through in the last two years, Charlie Seagram was only too eager to do something worthwhile for himself and the country, even if it meant chancing death at the hands of a cruel, ruthless enemy.

'The unit was started by a naval wallah called Willmott, somewhere in the Middle East. They tell me he'd already won the DSO and DSC by 1943. I never came across him, though he and his blokes did the preliminary stuff for the bloody Salerno beach cock-up.' He frowned at what was obviously a bad memory of the invasion of Italy below Rome. 'But I waffle, Seagram. Willmott started off with a bunch of swimmers launched from subs to check out beach defences – secretly. Since then, the pilotage people have developed their techniques to take in collecting samples of sand, measuring beach gradients, probing for dangerous rocks and shoals – all the stuff that General Eisenhower, the Supreme Commander, has needed to know for the coming invasion. They've been at it for months now and I've heard on the grapevine, as the Yanks say, that the op is so secret that when one of the pilotage failed to make his rendezvous with the sub that had taken him to France, he deliberately swam out to sea and drowned himself rather than be taken by the Hun and give the great secret away.' Ferguson was abruptly very sombre. 'That takes a hell of a lot of courage, Seagram, don't you think?'

The latter nodded. Quietly he said, 'I don't think I could do that, sir.'

Ferguson hesitated a moment before saying, equally quietly, 'Neither do I – and they couldn't even give him a gong for his courage or tell his people how he had died so bravely.' He shook his head. 'The COPP people are really the tops. Now I want you to come with me using their men. But I want to ask you now, and please give me a straight answer, Charlie – I think we better use our first names now. Mine's Peter. Can you cope with it?'

'Yessir, er, Peter. I can cope. I'm a fair swimmer, I can handle a small boat. Yes – can do. But what exactly is the role I am supposed to play in this business? It's been puzzling me ever since I became one of your bigots, Peter.'

Ferguson didn't seem to hear his question. Instead, he said, 'Come on, Charlie. Hop in the car. I'll drive you back to camp. Bit of a wash-and-brush-up and I'll buy you a drink in the mess, if you fancy one.'

It was a test and Seagram knew it. He realized his old reputation had preceded him. He'd heard the snide remarks made about 'Seagram's Gin' and the like. So he answered, 'Not tonight, er, Peter. I think I wouldn't mind walking back to camp. I'd like to think things over.'

'Understood. Good show, Charlie.' Surprisingly the colonel held out his hand. Seagram shook it. It was as if some kind of bond had just been sealed.

Two

Charlie Seagram was in a pensive mood, though he was mildly happy, too, as he walked along the deserted clifftop road towards the camp. In the icy spectral light of the moon which had now risen, he might well have been the last man alive in the world. The fact didn't worry him. He was glad of the silence and the loneliness. It gave him a chance to think things out.

It was now over a month since he had touched a real drink. It had been tough, very tough at first. But then when the desire for booze had almost overcome him, he had thought of how those dying sailors had looked in the water as the cruiser had sunk, and the disgusted look on the flotilla leader's face as he snapped, 'There won't be a court of inquiry. Churchill has ordered the whole matter to be kept a close secret till after the war – and by then no one will be interested. But I'm firing that sot of a skipper of yours, and you've been transferred from my flotilla as of this day. I won't have my sailors put at risk by drunken swine like you, Seagram.'

Seagram had felt himself flush violently. He had been so ashamed of himself. At that moment he prayed fervently that a hole would appear in the floor of the flotilla leader's office and swallow him up. But that wasn't to be. The lieutenant commander's eyes had flashed fire and he had cried, 'Churchill or no Churchill, if I had my way you'd be cashiered and dismissed from the service tomorrow morning. You knew about your skipper. You should have either helped him to get off that damned bottle or reported him to the authorities, who would have done. But you didn't because you're like him yourself, an addict. Now both of you have the lives of good honest British seamen on your conscience – for ever!'

The words had stabbed home like the blade of a sharp knife. He had felt himself tremble as if he might faint at any moment, and it had been only with an effort of sheer willpower that he had been able to retain his balance.

'Well, it's over as far as I'm concerned, Seagram,' the flotilla leader had concluded, the bitterness in his voice only too apparent. 'You'll never get a chance to kill anyone else. I'm having you posted to the tugs and I hope they'll keep you working your arse off towing stinking cargo ships in and out of harbours for the rest of your naval career, and then when the war is over the authorities will get rid of you as soon as damned possible. The Royal Navy can do without your kind. All right, dismiss. Get out of my sight!' He had bent his head to his papers as if Seagram didn't exist.

How he had got out of that office, Seagram didn't know. But the shame of it all had remained with him ever since. Even now the very thought of it made his cheeks burn, as if he had been struck by a sudden fever. 'But now you've got a chance – a last chance,' a tiny voice at the back of his mind said encouragingly. He looked at the lonely road ahead, and for a moment it seemed to symbolize his own position. He was alone in the world really. The admiral, Bert, and Peter Ferguson had certainly done their best to encourage him to make a new start of things. But, in reality, it was up to him to make a go of it; he couldn't afford to muck things up again. He'd never get a second chance, he knew that implicitly.

Involuntarily he clenched his fists as if he were about to tackle a vicious enemy when he was startled by the sound of a cycle bell and a female voice saying, 'Heaven help a sailor on a dark night like this. You'll go and get yourself run over if you don't take more care, Lieutenant.'

He turned and in the icy light of the moon he recognized one of the Salvation Army girls who had served 'char and wads' to the troops at the end of the last exercise. He recalled her from the afternoon as jolly and pretty with a broad generous mouth set in a genuine smile as she humoured the squaddies, who in the manner of soldiers everywhere made the usual sexual advances. 'Hello,' he said, glad of the interruption in his train of thought. 'The bobbies will fine you if they catch you riding with that light not blacked out.'

She laughed easily. 'The bobbies'll have to catch me first. Besides, the only one I know is probably already down at the Malt Shovel trying to cadge a free half-pint before the pub runs out of beer with all you thirsty servicemen.'

He shared her laugh. 'Well, young lady, you'd better be on your way.'

'I'll give you a lift if you're going back to the camp. I pass it on my way to band practice.'

'Band practice?'

'Yes, I play the flute in the Sally Ann silver band. Great honour, you know. They've only started taking us poor hopeless females into the silver band because the men were called up.' She laughed again and he told himself the young Sally Ann girl seemed to laugh a lot, and that it was good that there were people like her, who could still laugh.

'You said give me a lift. On your bike?'

'Of course. What else?'

Seagram, standing there in the moonlight on the lonely coastal road, was suddenly embarrassed. It seemed years now since he had been alone with a decent girl. She seemed to feel his embarrassment, for she said, laughing again, 'You don't need to worry, Lieutenant. You're safe with me. After all I

121

am a Sally Ann lass.'

He smiled. 'All right, I'll take a chance. But where do I sit?'

'Behind me on the pillion, naturally. Come on. If I don't get home on time my old dad will read me the riot act. He's a home guard, you know.'

Seagram was too busy attempting to get behind her without touching her back to wonder about the relevance of her father being in the Home Guard. Finally, he managed it, but before she set off again, raising herself on one pedal, she ordered, 'Put your arm around my waist, Lieutenant. I don't want you falling off. I know just how awkward you men are.'

Gingerly he did so, and felt the youthful softness of her body and sensed her fragrance, which seemed as natural as the summer flowers themselves. Then they were off to a clumsy zigzag start, so that he clutched her waist even more to prevent falling off, experiencing a feeling of desire he hadn't known for these many long months.

She stopped just outside the guard house and the sentry box, where a sentry looked at them a little suspiciously in the faint blue light above the barbed wire and sandbags.

'Well?' she asked a little breathlessly, 'how

did I do – with your weight?'

He wasn't offended. Indeed he was rather pleased, especially as the sentry was now looking at him enviously. He said, 'Very well. If you could see your way to it, miss, I'd like to try it again.'

'Don't "miss" me,' she answered a little sharply. 'Lorna's my name – after Lorna Doone. I think it was the only book my mother read at her council school. And yes, we can do it again, as long as I don't have to keep calling you Lieutenant.'

'Charlie Seagram,' he answered.

'Like the gin,' she commented.

'Like the gin,' he echoed, telling himself that this innocent Salvation Army girl little realized just how close she had come to the truth about him with her comment.

Quite formally they shook hands. She said, 'You'll find me at the Citadel, Charlie Seagram.' Then she was gone, pedalling hard up the hill that led from the camp, while he presented his officer's card to the sentry, to be told, 'Colonel Ferguson's left a message for you, sir, in the guardroom.'

He had. It read simply, 'We're off to see the Wizard, Charlie. Zero six hundred hours tomorrow morning. Pleasant dreams. Peter F.'

And that night, for once, Charlie Seagram did have pleasant dreams...

He awoke feeling fresh and slightly happy. He told himself he felt that way on account of the chance meeting with the girl from the Sally Ann. But he knew it was due, too, to the fact that he hadn't been on the booze the night before. For years, it seemed, he had woken up feeling liverish, dull and head-achy. Now things were changing.

Outside the morning was fresh and sunny. It already felt as if it was going to be hot later in the day. All around him there was the sound of an army camp in wartime waking up: the rattle of tea dixies at the cookhouse; the bugler marching stiffly across the parade ground ready to sound reveille; the orderly sergeant with his red sash and armband standing at the door of the first Nissen hut preparing to fling open the door and shout at the sleep-dazed soldiers inside, 'All right, me lucky lads. Out of them bunks. Hands off yer cocks and on with yer socks'; weary jankers men marching in single file behind a regimental policeman, heading for the cook-house and spud bashing as the first of their day's punishment.

Seagram took it all in, feeling that new sense of purpose; a feeling that he belonged to something that was carrying him forward to a recognizable objective, even though that objective might well mean death for many of those young men now waking from a too-short sleep – and perhaps for him, too.

'Penny for 'em.' It was Ferguson, looking bathed and fresh and carrying two haversacks.

Automatically he clicked to attention, then thought better of it, saying, 'Good morning, Peter. Just enjoying the morning air, that's all.'

'Here,' Ferguson slung him one of the haversacks, 'rations, for one, bully beef doorstep and one of jam. The cook's idea of a balanced diet. And a map. You're a naval officer, Charlie. You're doing the map reading.'

'Map reading?'

'Yes, we're going cross-country to some place near Poole. You're guiding us there.' He smiled winningly. 'Rank hath its privileges, you know, Charlie. Colonels don't map-read. Lowly lieutenants do. Come on. The fifteen hundredweight is waiting.'

Five minutes later, Ferguson at the wheel and Seagram with the map spread on his knees, they were seated in the cab of the draughty truck heading south-west. For a while they concentrated on driving down empty roads that were devoid of any road sign, through silent villages and little towns bare of traffic save for the occasional army vehicle. Once, they passed a convoy of American troops pulled over to one side, the men fast asleep in the ditches, with no one seemingly awake or on his feet save for a solitary white-helmeted military policeman who moved them on in a lazy, bored manner. He didn't even salute Ferguson.

Ferguson shook his head. 'Bad business,' he muttered, as if to himself.

'Because he didn't salute you, Peter?'

'Christ no. Because the Yanks didn't have any sentries out. Imagine a set-up like that in the field. Some Hun armed with a machine pistol would slaughter the bloody lot of 'em in five minutes flat.' He shook his head again. 'Before this do is over, Charlie, we're going to have trouble with our cousins from across the sea – mark my words.'

Immediately after this he forgot the Americans and their lack of precautions. As the road ceased its windings and was outlined dead straight in front of him so that he could relax a little at the wheel, Colonel Ferguson said, 'Tell me something about tugs, Charlie.'

Coming completely out of the blue, the question caught Charlie Seagram by surprise. 'Tugs?'

'Yes, bloody tugs, Charlie. You command one. Indeed, you've commanded one for a very long time. Now tell me about 'em.'

Seagram thought Ferguson's request was a bit of a tall order, but he tried his best. He explained what tugs were supposed to do, going from general information to such details as the 'ten bollard pull' and 'twelve pax in the wheelhouse'. Ferguson listened patiently, though it was obvious to Seagram that he didn't understand half of what was being said. About ten they stopped by the roadside and had their haversack lunch, washed down with a thermosful of coffee – the first coffee that Seagram had drunk for months. It was when they had finished the 'cook's doorsteps', as Ferguson called them, that he asked his question, which gave Seagram his first clue to what the engineer officer was really trying to find out.

'Charlie, could you give me the draft of the average tug – and perhaps its beam, too?' He smiled at the other man.

Charlie Seagram frowned. 'Well, I can. But first of all you need to know what the draft limit is.'

'You mean the maximum allowable draft in feet, as assigned by the Admiralty? The distance at the bow and stern between the waterline and keel that serves as a guide against overloading in connection with the strength or ability of the tug to survive underwater damage?'

Seagram stared at Ferguson open mouthed. 'Why, you bugger, if you'll forgive my French. You've been leading me up the bloody garden path all the while, haven't you?'

'Not exactly. But I just wanted to hear your thoughts in general. But back to draft and beam.'

'Well, Peter, as you probably know – as you seem to know everything already, I'm not in deep-sea tugs. I can only speak of the close-shore ones like the one I command.'

'Go on.'

'Mine's a former US tug, transferred to us under Roosevelt's Lease-Lend Agreement of 1941. Ideal for coastal work because she's got a wooden hull and—'

'Can dodge mines and the like,' Ferguson beat him to it. 'And her beam, Charlie?'

'About eighteen foot, I'd say, off hand.'

'Excellent.' Now Ferguson's hard blue eyes were gleaming as if with excitement. 'Draft.'

Puzzled as ever, Seagram answered, 'I'm sure you know already, but you're testing me to find out whether *I* know.'

Ferguson didn't rise to the bait. Instead, he waited expectantly, standing there at the side of the deserted road, thermos flask in his hand.

'Approximately twenty feet, Peter.'

'Splendid, Charlie. It's exactly what I've been hoping for all along, ever since the admiral – your Bert – recommended you for this job.' Before Seagram could ask what the job was, Ferguson thrust his thermos back into his small pack and said, 'Remember that bloody bunker I told you about?'

A puzzled Seagram nodded.

'Well, we think we've found a way to get to it. Now we'll find out. Hurry up, Charlie, remember we're off to see the Wizard.' Suddenly he burst out into the song from *The Wizard of Oz* that everyone had been singing four years earlier, when the world had still seemed so innocent. 'We're off to see the Wizard ... the wonderful Wizard of Oz...' Seagram shook his head and then he followed.

Three

The 'Wizard' was waiting for them at the little naval camp set just above the sea's high-tide line. He was watching some of his men handling a bright new canoe, occasionally bending to poke the fabric or handling the paddles, as if he were testing them for weight and balance. Behind him, leaning against one of the camouflaged Nissen huts, three Wrens were busy sticking contraceptives on the end of broom poles, and when they were fully extended, powdering the rubber sheaths carefully. Their young and pretty faces revealed nothing; they were not even grinning at their sexually explicit act. Nor did the motley crew of sailors and soldiers who passed them as they gave the powdered contraceptives to another Wren, who equally carefully rolled them up again.

Ferguson looked at Seagram. The other repeated the puzzled look, for he had absolutely no idea why the Wrens should be employed powdering the contraceptives in public. Ferguson cleared his throat. The Wizard, as they would always call him privately, turned swiftly. Both of them noticed his hand fall to his belt, in which he had tucked a revolver of some foreign make. Again the two visitors had no idea why he should be carrying the weapon, and in such an unorthodox manner.

'Commander Willmott?' Ferguson asked.

'That's right. You're Ferguson and this is, I suppose, Lieutenant Seagram?'

They nodded, and before attempting to shake hands or salute, for Ferguson was the senior in rank there, Willmott looked at them with his dreamy grey eyes set in a rawbone face, which like his body seemed pared down and devoid of any fat. He looked like a man who had been in training for years, which he was. The Wizard might look dreamy and move in a strange awkward fashion, Seagram told himself, but he was damned fit all the same.

The Wizard smiled. 'Come on over to the wardroom. We'll have a drink?' He hesitated. 'Or a cup of tea if you would rather have that disgusting liquid.' He looked at Seagram and he knew that the Wizard also knew about his problem. He felt himself beginning to flush with embarrassment. But

Ferguson said quickly, 'Tea would suit us fine.'

The Wizard shrugged carelessly. 'Well, there's no accounting for tastes. Come on.' Without waiting for them he set off in his strange awkward gait. As he passed the Wrens they didn't rise in the presence of their commanding officer. Nor were they embarrassed by these strange officers watching them busy at their bizarre task.

'Used with our beach augur. Decant the sand into the french letter. Tells us the sand bearing capacity when we get the sample back home.'

Neither of the two visitors understood a word of what the Wizard was talking about. But it didn't matter; Ferguson had heard that not many people, even scientists involved in the secrets of the COPP parties, knew what the Wizard talked about.

They passed into the 'wardroom', half a Nissen hut with a makeshift bar, a ship's wheel on the wall and a bullet-scarred road sign in German stating s halten an der kreuzung ist streng verboten t !

The Wizard saw the direction of their gaze. Cheerfully, as soon as he had finished his order to the wardroom steward, who wore gumboots and a battered jersey with holes at the elbows, he explained, 'It means don't stop at the crossing. Nicked it from one of the coastal railways the Jerries have put up at their Atlantic Wall to bring up supplies and the like. Nicked one like it just before the war. It said, "The chamberpot finds itself under the bed". Blasted to kingdom come when the Jerries bombed Pompey in '40.'

The Wizard waited for the scruffy mess steward to pass the other two officers a huge bowl full of lumps of sugar, showing that this unorthodox little secret unit didn't take the armed forces' rationing system very seriously, then he said, 'All right, Pongo, sling yer hook.'

'Ay ay, sir,' the steward said cheerfully, 'I'll be behind the wardroom door aft, if yer need me, sir.'

The Wizard sighed, lifted his glass in toast, drank a great slug and commenced business straightaway. 'Monty's having kittens. He doesn't like the idea of our messing about on the beaches that we and the Yanks are going to invade. Can understand his point. But without us, no invasion, what?'

Like everything else here, his statement puzzled them, but they both agreed. It seemed the wisest course of action with the Wizard, inpatient and energetic as he was.

'So, the Master, as we call Monty, wants us to cut down our little jaunts to foreign parts, i.e. the beaches. It looks, therefore, Ferguson, as if we can only do you one trip on the old *Skylark* across the Channel.'

Ferguson nodded his understanding, but said nothing. He knew the Wizard by now. He didn't take kindly to interruptions when he was in full flow, as he was at the moment.

'Now, we've ascertained already,' the Wizard continued, 'that there is a little channel that runs right to about fifty yards from that damned bunker of yours, Colonel Ferguson. We've also worked with the aid of the bong stick, "rod sounding gear" is how it's listed in navy parlance. You understand, Colonel?'

'No, I'm afraid I don't, Commander.' Ferguson decided he'd chance his arm and interrupt at this stage.

'Oh, it's an iron rod. You lower it into the old briney, give it a bloody great whack with a hammer and the noise can be picked up up to, at the most, twelve miles off shore.'

'A signalling device then,' Ferguson said.

'Exactly. You engineer wallahs are quick off the mark.' The Wizard smiled. 'So once the paddlers are in position they can signal to the sub where exactly they are without all those flashing lights and torch signals which are a dead giveaway to any watching sentry. So,' he attempted to sum up, 'we can get our chaps in and out and we know where the channel is even when the beaches are covered at high tide.' He paused momentarily to let his words sink in. 'What we don't know is the strength of the sand on both sides of the channel to the bunker and whether they would collapse if they were hit by the sides of some larger craft than our canoes.' He looked significantly at Seagram.

Slowly an unpleasant thought was beginning to uncurl in Seagram's mind; it was like a serpent unwinding itself and baring its poison fangs, ready to strike. 'Larger craft', the Wizard had said. What kind of larger craft did he mean? Was his fate going to be linked to that vessel? It seemed to Seagram, there could be no other role he could fulfil in this strange business. 'So we'll have to go in. This time it will be you, Ferguson, again, and our new boy, Lieutenant Seagram here. Hope you can swim, Lieutenant.' It was the same question that Ferguson had asked. He nodded he could but made no comment.

'Good show,' the Wizard said. 'So it will be sub, canoe – the new one you saw as you came in – and, if you're out of luck, swimming. You've got twenty-four hours to train with the chaps who will take you in. Not much, I know, but with Monty making very threatening noises, I don't think—'

He didn't finish, for at that moment there was a knock at the wardroom door. 'Enter,' the Wizard called.

It was the scruffy wardroom steward, bearing a small box. 'For you, sir,' he announced. 'Special messenger from Montgomery's HQ in Portsmouth.'

'What is it?' the Wizard demanded.

'Don't rightly like to say, sir.'

'What the bloody hell is that supposed to mean?'

By way of an answer, the scruffy sailor handed the box hastily to his CO as if it were red hot.

The Wizard took it and then laughed out loud when he read the inscription. 'Do you know what these are, gents,' he exclaimed in high good humour, as if he had just read something very funny. 'Instant Death Pills.' He screwed up his eyes and read the notice in red below. 'To be ... taken ... with discretion. Ha, ha. Oh my sainted aunt – *to be taken with discretion*. What next? But then there would be no "next", would there?'

Neither Ferguson nor Seagram was amused. Outside a soldier started to sing in a mournful voice, 'Kiss me goodnight, Sergeant Major, tuck me in my little wooden bed ... We all love you, Sergeant Major.'

Ferguson shook his head as if in mock wonder. 'Kiss me good night, *indeed...*'

The next twenty-four hours passed in hectic activity for the two visitors. Ferguson had already familiarized himself with the drill and the kit, but he went through it again on Seagram's behalf. He wanted to be quite sure that the junior officer knew the standard operating procedure thoroughly, for not only did their own lives depend upon it, but perhaps those of thousands of soldiers some time shortly in the future.

In response to their unspoken questions – 'What if the assault boats do manage to hit the right beach from eight miles out – what sort of beach are they going to find to land on? Does air recce or periscope sketches made from a sub tell us where the beach shelves nicely? How do we know where to dodge sandbars, rocks, soft sand patches?' – the Wizard's response had been 'That's our job, gentlemen. Now let us look at what we've got...'

What they were to receive for their mission was obviously equipment that had been evolved through trial-and-error by the

137

Wizard and his COPP teams. There was an army compass – 'borrowed before it was lost,' as the Wizard explained gleefully – covered with periscope grease so that it could operate at a depth of fifteen feet; a torch covered with a couple of contraceptives to make it waterproof at depths. As Ferguson commented sotto voce to Seagram, 'Wonder what Stores think of the number of contraceptives this little lot indents for.' Seagram laughed. 'Perhaps they're all sex-mad down here.'

The clothing they would wear for their visit to the Normandy beach was also clearly based on the old trial and-error method. It consisted of a long white pullover of the type used by submariners, but soaked heavily in grease; the long white underpants, 'drawers, long, sailors for the use of', were similarly heavily doused in grease, which, as the Wizard declared with a naughty wink, would 'tickle yer fancy if nothing else'. Over this went a clumsy wetsuit made of thick black rubber, with a little pocket at the waist, together with a helmet and goggles.

'That's where you put your L-Pill,' the Wizard informed them. 'And don't ask me to explain to you what the "L-Pill" is.' But they already knew. 'L' stood for 'lethal'. As they had already been told by the scruffy wardroom steward, 'If yer think you're not gonna come back, it's better to swallow it, gents, and snuff it straight away.'

Once their gear had been demonstrated and they had tried on the awkward wetsuits, they were shown how to get into the canoes once they had been lowered into the sea by the submarine's crew. Their two paddlers, brawny young seamen whose shoulder and arm muscles rippled like snakes every time they moved their bodies, explained with the professional casualness of men who had carried out the drill many a time off enemy coasts. 'First thing, you make as little noise as possible, gentlemen. At night, with a relatively calm sea, you'd be surprised how far even the slightest sound carries.'

They nodded and waited till Andy, the bigger of the two paddlers, got ready to demonstrate how they should get into the canoe once the submariners had launched it. He and his mate, Hector, another tough-looking muscular Scot, had found a patch of calm sea in one of the coves that bordered the little camp. Now the canoe bobbed up and down on the wavelets, as Andy said, 'Now, there's a right and a wrong way, gentlemen, of getting into a canoe of this type. First I'll show ye the wrong way.'

Seagram, who had done some work with canoes before the war during those peacetime weekends of 'mucking about in boats' on the Solent, watched as Andy rested his big hands on the canoe's fabric on both sides of the little craft's cockpit. He gave a small push and raised himself upwards almost effortlessly. The canoe moved away slightly under the water and Andy hit the sea again with a splash. 'Wrong way,' he said. 'Why? I'll tell ye. A noise and a white splash of water that any attentive beach sentry might hear or see. Dead giveaway.' He raised his voice. 'Hector gie's a hand.'

The other Scot waded to the front of the little craft, placed his hands on it and steadied the canoe. Andy waited. 'Now ye've seen them Yankee pictures no doubt, where Tom Mix or yon Gene Autry gets on his horse. That's the way we do it.' Even as he finished his explanation he had placed his hands on the back of the canoe, drawn a sharp breath and vaulted like a cowboy might on to a wild mustang, right into the cockpit. Next moment he had the paddle in his grasp, ready to go.

Exhausted and stiff that night, Seagram

squatted in one of the leather armchairs that was the only kind of comfort provided in the spartan little wardroom. On the radio, Vera Lynn was warbling as usual about meeting again, while Ferguson drank his pint of beer in silence and the Wizard had his head bent over his sketchpad, working out some technical problem or other (the Wizard never seemed able to sit still; he was trying out new ideas and techniques constantly).

To Seagram, drinking the warm lemonade provided by the scruffy steward, who was still wearing his battered gumboots for some reason, it was a scene that was almost domestic rather than one of men who might well die on the morrow – violently. Despite the knowledge that this was so, Seagram felt happy here and in the company of these brave men.

Then for a moment he forgot the little scene around him and remembered Lorna, the Sally Ann girl who played the flute in the Salvation Army Silver Band. She had said the last time they had met that he could find her through the 'Citadel', but he hadn't the foggiest idea where the Sally Ann headquarters was. Had she said that just to get rid of him? he wondered. Somehow he didn't think she had. She didn't look like the kind of girl who would tell fibs. All the same, she had mentioned her Home Guard father, who was very strict. Perhaps she was trying to keep him at arm's distance for the sake of peace and quiet in the old family home?

It was the Wizard who broke into his thoughts, as he lifted his head from his sketching and said mysteriously, 'Well, gentlemen, I think it's time to hit the hay. We've got a long day in front of us tomorrow and we'll need our wits about us – and then some – if we don't want to end up in Rose Cottage, what?'

Ferguson looked puzzled. 'Rose Cottage?' he queried, as Vera Lynn continued to warble about star-crossed lovers.

The Wizard grinned. 'That's what we call exitus, Ferguson. The mortuary.'

Ferguson shared his grin, but with no great enthusiasm. 'Roses around the door, old folks dream, eh. Very clever.' He put out his pipe.

Seagram frowned, and the thoughts of the girl from the Sally Ann vanished immediately. He guessed that before all this was over he might well end up in the Wizard's 'Rose Cottage'. Outside the wind began to howl and the one window rattled noisily in its metal frame. It seemed a storm was brewing.

142

Four

About 3.00 that May morning, the little submarine broke surface and started to charge her batteries. The thrumming noise the chargers made, as the matelots unloaded the canoes, seemed deafening, and Ferguson kept looking anxiously at the dark smudge on the horizon that was France. But all was silent. They obviously hadn't been heard.

On the deck, the Wizard, who had insisted on going with them in the second canoe, was busy applying tan boot polish to his face. Seagram, doing the same, couldn't help thinking his companion was doing so with all the attentiveness of a vain girl applying her make-up. In the faint light from the interior of the sub his mouth gaped pink and his teeth glowed like pearls. He finished, and, swallowing the benzedrine tablets they would all take to keep them at top alertness for the long task to come, the Wizard whispered, 'Cheers.'

'Cheers,' Seagram whispered back, and

realized he hadn't used that particular toast for a long time now; the thought made him feel good.

Now the sub started to move closer to the shore once more, the batteries nearly charged.

'Half ahead both ... Port fifteen,' the skipper called softly. From the engine room came the answer.

'Both engines ahead ... Fifteen o'port, sir.' Now a slight swell slapped the craft's bow. It was the only noise save the soft smooth purr of the electric motors. 'Steer three-three-nine,' the skipper called down his voice tube. 'Open forehatch, please.' There was a rusty creaking as the hatch to the torpedo compartment was opened and the second canoe was pushed on to the gleaming wet deck to be swiftly assembled.

For a little while longer they ploughed on, with the lookouts' gaze fixed hypnotically on the land ahead: Hitler's *Festung Europa*, where every man's hand was against them. At four miles off shore, the little submarine stopped engines once more. This time hardly a command was given. They were on silent running. Seagram clambered over the bridge and down the ladder past the gun platform. Here the two ratings manning the four-inch quick-firer stood like statues, rigid, taut and unseeing as he passed.

On the casing two seamen lay full-length, appearing not to notice the waves that washed over them, trying to suck them into the sea as they held on to the Wizard's canoe, in which he was going to guide them in. Behind them the others waited.

The sea was thickening. The two men were having difficulty holding the canoe steady as it bobbed and yawped. The Wizard, however, didn't hesitate. He vaulted on to it and landed correctly the first time. The canoe bucked and rose wildly like a horse being put to the saddle for the first time. But the Wizard, expert that he was, held on. Next moment he was handed his paddle and tommy gun, and with a delicate sweep of the former he moved away in a flurry of white and waited for the others to come after him.

Ferguson and Seagram had it easier. They were being accompanied by the other two experts, the Scots, Andy and Hector. Almost immediately they were aboard they dug their double-bladed paddles into the swell and moved off. Behind them the submarine started its electric motors once more and moved away before diving. They were alone with the sea and the enemy coast ahead...

They worked easily together, paddling side by side in a long swinging rhythm. Now and again they moved into a pitch of heavy swell. Then the canoes corkscrewed, slithering sideways into a hollow, the waves slapping noisily against the sides and the wind peppering their blackened faces with cold spray. Seagram didn't know about the others, but he felt it exhilarating: a challenge; a test of his new-found self. All the same, concerned as he was with himself, he realized the imminent danger.

To their front now, they could see the dark mass of the coast more clearly, with the crenellations of the buildings that made up the coastal villages, which would be the first targets of the Iron Division once they had cleared the beaches. *If*, a hard little voice at the back of Seagram's head rasped. He dismissed the voice and concentrated on his task.

He and Ferguson – and their two paddlers, too, probably – were sweating heavily inside their greased woollens. Seagram could feel the sweat trickling icily down the small of his spine with each movement of his shoulders as he worked his double-bladed paddle. But again he felt a sense of achievement even with all this hard labour. At last he was doing something worthwhile and important again.

To their front the Wizard stopped. The others did the same. He unhooked his masked torch, the french letters still holding out against the waves. While he consulted the sketches he had made through the sub's periscope, the others rested bent backed over their paddles and stared at the village to their front, silhouetted against what looked like large rocks, but which they knew were the bunkers meant to protect them from assault from the sea. The place was as quiet as the grave. Not a chink of light showed. Nor was there a single sound. France, it seemed, had well and truly gone to sleep for the night. It was something for which they were all grateful, for they knew what their fate would be if they were caught now. They'd be beaten to all hell and when that was over they'd be lined up against the nearest wall and shot out of hand.

The Wizard rose slightly in his cockpit. He indicated the direction with his gloved hand. They turned slightly to starboard and, in single file, recommenced paddling behind him, trying to keep as low a silhouette as possible. Quiet the place might be, but they were taking no chances.

Gently they slid their paddles through the water. They didn't want to stir up any phosphorescence that might attract the attention of a German sentry. All the time they stared at the little village, but it was eerily void of life. The only sound was that of the fishing boats stirring at their moorings.

Now they were riding on a very gentle swell. Seagram guessed there was less than three feet of water beneath them. A moment or two later he knew his guess was right, as the Wizard, in the lead, relinquished his paddle and slithered into the water, while Ferguson and his paddler held on to his canoe. A slight splash and the Wizard was heading for the white cord which was the surf against the rocks of the shore. Andy hissed to Seagram in a stage whisper, 'You now, sir.'

Seagram didn't hesitate. He gave a swift twist about as he had been taught the previous day and lay across the canoe. While Andy leaned his bulk the other way, he slithered into the water. He gasped with shock. Hot as he was from paddling, the water seemed freezing in contrast. He hung on to the side, trying to catch his breath. Andy didn't give him a chance. 'Awa ye go,' he commanded in his broad Scots. 'Ye ken the CO's a-waiting.'

Seagram nodded. For a moment he couldn't speak. He started to breaststroke to where the Wizard crouched in the shingle. A moment later Ferguson followed. A few minutes afterwards they were crouched, all three of them surveying ahead of them, with the silent village to their right.

The Wizard whistled softly as his eyes became accustomed to the darkness. 'We were right. There is a channel leading up to where the bunker should be. What do you think, Charlie?'

Seagram tried to stop his teeth chattering. 'Well, it's broad enough, I think,' he answered. 'But—'

'Freeze!' The Wizard cut him off urgently.

They froze. About twenty yards away at the little concrete slipway, probably used by the village's fishing smacks, there was the sudden outline of a helmeted figure, and there was no mistaking that coal-scuttle helmet. It belonged to a German soldier. Heart pounding frantically like a trip hammer, Seagram tried not to move a single muscle, for he hoped that all of them would look like part of the rocky outcrop. Suddenly he heard himself praying fervently: the first time he had done so since he had left school,

149

in what seemed another age. The German was turning his head in their direction and the three trapped men could hear another voice speaking in German close to the first sentry. There were two of them, both armed with rifles slung over their shoulders.

How long they lay there in the freezing shallows, Seagram could never work out afterwards, but it seemed an age. Once, the first German turned his head in their direction, and stared long and hard at the 'rocks'. The slight breeze coming across the beach now seemed to cut through Seagram's suit so that his very skin appeared to shrink and tighten, and he clenched his teeth to keep from trembling and his teeth from chattering, till his jaw ached.

Then Seagram caught the words *'Kaffee'* and *'Jawohl, jetzt'*. At that moment he would dearly have loved to sigh with relief, but he daren't. It seemed the two Germans were going away for coffee. In the end they did so, tramping noisily up the ramp until the sound of their hobnailed boots disappeared into the night.

In a tiny voice, the Wizard said, 'Keeps you on your toes, doesn't it?'

'Toes? I don't think I've got any of the buggers left,' Ferguson snapped angrily. 'In fact,

I think I've got frostbite. Come on.'

'All sent to try us,' the Wizard replied placidly, and rose.

Now the three of them started to follow the stream, for that was what it was. Seagram tasted it gingerly. It was fresh water from the interior, not salty sea water, and it was even colder than the sea. At times they moved along the bank, testing the firmness of the sand on both sides. At others they swam and waded through the centre of the stream itself. The coldness of the fresh water seeped into Seagram's very bones until he was shivering desperately and it was an agony to move. What he could have given now for a hot rum, even a cold one, anything strong and alcoholic which would burn into his body and revive his flagging energy. But even as he longed for alcohol, he knew it was wrong. It would be backsliding, as the pretty little Sally Ann girl would undoubtedly have said.

So the freezing aching drudgery continued, not that the Wizard seemed to notice it. Every now and again he would stop and make notes on his special board with a chinagraph pencil, as if he were back in his little office and not on an enemy beach on the other side of the Channel in danger of being shot dead at any moment. Seagram shook his head in mock wonder. The Wizard was definitely a cool card.

Slowly but surely, despite the terrible cold, they progressed up the little coastal stream, knowing that their reconnaissance would have to end soon. For somewhere ahead in the inky darkness there was the bunker, just above the high water mark; and a bunker would be manned with alert Germans ready to start firing at the slightest suspicious sound. Already they'd spotted the rusting barbed wire on both sides of the stream, and where the waterline commenced they had noted what the Wizard had called 'Rommel's asparagus': a trestle-like arrangement of beams, with a mine or explosive charge balanced in top. As the Wizard had explained in a hurried whisper, 'At high tide they'll be just under the surface of the water. Any landing craft scraping its keel on one of those devilish devices won't be landing any troops, take my word for it.'

They did, and again Seagram noted just what valuable work the Wizard was carrying out, as he marked the position of this piece of Rommel's asparagus on his board before moving on again towards the still hidden bunker. The Wizard had got a couple of good gongs for his work in the Med already. Surely he deserved another for this job, which would probably remain secret even after the war was won.

They pushed on even further, though they knew dawn came early at this time of the year. But they were all aware of the importance of discovering whether the stream came within attacking distance of the bunker. Ten minutes later, with the sky to the east flushing the ugly white of the false dawn, they spotted it: a squat concrete structure, seeming barely to rise above ground level, ringed by barbed wire and with a sentry pacing the roof, machine pistol slung over his shoulder. There was something else, something which they might have easily missed, if the Wizard had not been looking specifically for this new danger.

'Halt,' he croaked urgently, holding up his right hand, as if to hold them back by force.

Something in his voice convinced the other two to do exactly that.

'What is it?' Ferguson asked hoarsely.

'Mines,' the Wizard hissed. 'Bouncing Bettys, I think.'

'What are they when they're at home?' Seagram heard himself ask, a nerve at the side of his frozen, ashen face beginning to tick urgently.

'Anti-personnel mines,' Ferguson answered, not taking his gaze off the damp grass in front of them. 'Three-pronged bastards. Step on one of them and Betty takes yer balls off.' He shuddered slightly. 'Nothing ladylike about those bastards.'

Seagram felt a cold finger of fear trace its way down his back. He shuddered too. In front of him, the Wizard whispered slowly, 'Back off – very slowly. Don't turn. Try to step in your own footsteps. I'll count to three. Then you move off, Peter. You're an engineer. You know the drill. I'll give you a minute and then it's your turn, Charlie.' For the first time he used Seagram's Christian name, and the latter realized that he was one of the team now. *'Three!'* the Wizard hissed.

'Moving,' Ferguson said. 'Now.' His voice was shaky.

Up on the roof of the bunker a light snapped on with startling suddenness. 'Bollocks,' the Wizard cursed. Next moment he ordered, 'Keep moving, Peter. Stop if the beam comes this way.'

'Roger,' Ferguson answered, and took his second step across the soggy grass.

On the roof of the bunker the other two could see the stark black outline of the sentry using the light. He was taking his time, flashing the beam in the direction of the village, as if he suspected whatever noise he had heard had been made by one of the villagers.

'Made it—' Ferguson stopped sharply and froze. The beam was coming their way.

'Standfast!' the Wizard broke in. They froze. Slowly the beam came ever closer, the soldier operator playing its icy white light up and down with too much thoroughness. Hastily the three men bent their heads and stood rigid, hardly daring to breathe.

And then it was on them, playing all about them and on their rigid bodies, so that abruptly their flesh seemed to be on fire, as if the beam were heating it. For an eternity it remained thus, while the three tensed expectantly for the first angry shout of warning and the high-pitched hysterical burst of Schmeisser fire.

But none came. An instant later the beam passed on, and then the Wizard retched, and his anxious stomach finally erupted and he vomited. Time and time again the vile spasms wracked his skinny body, and the cold sea air was suddenly filled with the nauseating stench of his outpourings...

Five

The three of them were completely exhausted, but they knew they had no time for a real rest. It was nearly dawn now, and they guessed the German coastal craft would soon be out along the Normandy coast. Before then they wanted to be in the sub and away. In the meantime, while the two Scots plied them with hot coffee and built a shelter-windbreak at the edge of the shore, the Wizard, recovered from his sickness, had begun attempting to use his 'bong stick' to signal the submarine in.

The iron rod made a tremendous noise, or so it seemed to a dog-tired Seagram, every time the Wizard struck it. But the Wizard didn't seem to notice. The others did. Every time the Wizard banged the iron rod stuck upright in the shallows, they jumped, even Seagram, who was drinking coffee that stung his mouth but which he couldn't feel, he was so cold.

Over at the village, there were the first stirrings of life as it grew lighter.

Here and there a reluctant boat motor coughed throatily as some sailor or other tried to get it to start. There was the clatter of wooden clogs on cobbles and the occasional phrase in French wafted their way on the breeze as sailors on the quay greeted each other with a thick morning, '*Ça va?*' and '*Va bien.*' Even an unutterably weary Seagram realized that time was running out – fast.

Then suddenly a dog started to bark. But this was not the bark of a pet. This was the harsh throaty sound of some large alert animal, outraged, insistent, attention-catching. It certainly caught the attention of its owner almost immediately. An equally harsh voice commanded, '*Sei doch ruhig, Lux ... Was ist denn los mit dem Koter?*'

The Wizard flashed Ferguson an alarmed look.

Ferguson nodded. 'Yes, German all right. It won't be long if that four-legged bugger keeps sounding the alarm like that. He's got our scent all right.'

The Wizard didn't hesitate. 'All right, Andy,' he commanded, 'get the bong stick. Come on, let's get mobile before they send some nosy parker sentry down here.'

The two Scots paddlers needed no urging.

They knew their lives were at stake. Swiftly they searched the little hide in the sand they had made for anything that, if left behind, would betray their presence. Then, while the Wizard pulled in the canoes, they destroyed the little structure and scuffed the sand with their boots to remove all telltale marks. The incoming tide would do the rest.

Over at the little port there were the sharp sounds of commands, the stamp of jack-boots and the first powerful roar of an engine starting up, sending the seagulls flying high into the dawn sky, crying in startled protest. But luck was apparently on the side of the intruders. In the same moment that they pushed off in their canoes and commenced paddling swiftly, the first of the mist began to creep in like a silent grey cat and wind itself around them. It appeared out of nowhere, coming in imperceptibly in faint wet wisps. It thickened rapidly, deadening the roar of that powerful engine back in the little fishing port.

With the mist the breeze dropped. Rapidly it changed into a pea-souper, blotting out their vision, deadening any sound so that they appeared to be gliding along almost noiselessly over the glass-smooth surface of the sea. But although they realized that the fog had appeared just at the right time, they knew they weren't safe yet – by a long chalk. The enemy knew they were there some-where, and the Germans didn't give up easily, the intruders realized that. Besides, although the fog had deadened virtually any sound they made with their paddles, it would be a different matter when the sub surfaced to pick them up. *If it ever does,* the hard little voice at the back of Seagram's mind warned sternly. He dismissed the voice and concentrated on his paddling. They would worry about that eventuality when it happened.

The benzedrine was beginning to wear off and Seagram found himself wearier than ever. He started to splash carelessly and a couple of times he found himself beginning to flounder, so that Andy in front of him turned and flashed him a warning glance. It meant keep the stroke. He bit his bottom lip till the blood came. The pain kept him alert for a while, but soon he started to flag once more. Now he prayed the submarine would surface and pick them up so that he could sleep – sleep for a whole day and then some.

Up in front the Wizard must have been experiencing the same feeling, for now he had unhooked his waterproof torch and, holding it high, swinging over the largest possible arc, he was flashing a morse 'R' seaward. But stubbornly there was no answering signal in green. The sub hadn't spotted them yet.

Time passed leadenly. The unseen, powerful German boat had passed through the entrance to the port – they had been able to hear the rattle of the boom chain being lowered. Now it was cruising round that general area slowly, trying to spot them. Occasionally, silver flares hissed into the dawn sky and hung there in their unreal incandescent beauty, trying to penetrate the fog. Without success so far. But a worried Wizard knew that the hunters would change course soon and come looking further afield, either to starboard or port, where they were. If that happened, he knew that there would be no other course for them than to fight to the death. With fingers that were virtually entirely numb now, he reached for his tommy gun and, with difficulty, clicked off the safety catch. It was a puny weapon against an armed German vessel, perhaps the search craft might even be a cannon-carrying Z-boat, but it was the only weapon he and the others had. They ploughed on doggedly, getting wearier by the minute.

The mist seemed to be thinning in parts now. Every so often the Wizard, still in the lead, could catch a glimpse of the North Star. That was a good sign, in a way, but also a bad one. If and when their pursuer changed direction to their starboard, he'd follow that same star, and then the inevitable, which the Wizard didn't like them to think about, would happen. He'd bump into the submarine come to pick them up. Were they then leading their rescuers into a trap? If they were, what should they – could they – do about it?

Five minutes later the mist seemed to have cleared altogether. One minute they were paddling through banks of mist as thick as a cloud, the next they were under a clear sky, visibility improving by the instant. The Wizard took a chance. He indicated by hand signals that the other two canoes should come in closer, with the men, now holding their tommy guns, forming a kind of a bodyguard. Hastily the Wizard handed over the bottle of whisky which he had kept for this moment. It had been meant to toast their success. Now its purpose was to bring some warmth back to his men's chilled bodies. Greedily they took their turn drinking from it, feeling the fiery spirits burn their way down their gullets, all save Seagram. He said thickly, 'You have my share, Andy.' The paddler needed no second invitation. He took a mighty swig and passed the Scotch on to Ferguson, who murmured so that the others couldn't hear, 'Good show, Charlie.' That praise did Seagram more good than the whisky might.

'Thanks, Peter,' he replied.

Stiffly the Wizard started to flash the recovery signal: an Aldis lamp with an infra-red screen. Behind him now, Ferguson trained the receiver, shaped like a clumsy box camera, and moved it across the surface of the sea, watching for the submarine's signal to appear as a green light on the apparatus's screen.

Suddenly there it was. A flashing spot appeared on the horizon to port.

'Got it,' Ferguson cried in triumph.

Around him the weary men could have cheered. It meant the end of their ordeal.

'Flash a bit further to port, Peter,' the Wizard ordered as they heard the first slow wash of the submarine's motors as she started for them over the still water.

Andy, the strongest of them all, was suddenly happy. Tonelessly he started to sing softly, 'Now this is number two and he's got it up me flue ... roll me over and do it again ... Roll me over in the clover.' Despite their weariness, the others grinned. They felt the same sense of relief. They were going to pull it off after all. With a bit of luck they'd soon be eating fried eggs, real ones, and bacon and perhaps a bit of fried bread thrown in. 'Now this is number four and he's got me on the floor—'

The roar drowned the rest of the bawdy army song.

Catching them totally, completely by surprise, the old fashioned Dornier flying boat fell out of the sky directly above them. If anything, they had expected to be ambushed by the German motor boat out there somewhere still searching for them in the mist to their rear. But not this enemy flying boat. Now it was skimming across the mirror-smooth surface of the sea, its gunner swinging his machine gun round to blow them out of the water.

Surprised as he was, the Wizard reacted correctly. 'Fire – everybody,' he yelled above the racket raised by the Dornier. 'Fire at will. For God's sake, open fire, chaps!'

Hurriedly, nerves ticking electrically, the men in the canoes balanced themselves the best they could and raised their tommy guns. The seaplane came roaring in at sea level. The noise was deafening. Below, it churned up the sea into a white boiling fury with its prop wash. The COPP men didn't seem to notice. They concentrated on their target. They knew their very lives just might depend on knocking the Dornier out of the sky, for already the submarine was on its way, gliding through the water towards them.

It had been a long time since Seagram had been on a firing range. Now he tried desperately to remember what the instructor had told him. Calm your breathing ... no hasty pulling at the trigger ... Smooth pull ... first and second pressure...

Even as he briefed himself with that long-forgotten lore, the Thompson sub-machine burst into frantic life. Its butt slammed painfully into his right shoulder and nearly knocked him over. His nostrils were assailed by the burnt stink of cordite. The blast slapped him across the face. It took the air from his lungs. He gasped for breath in the very same instant that the Dornier started to splutter and cough. Dark black smoke started to stream from its ruptured engine. A ragged cheer rose. He had hit the German plane!

Desperately, the pilot tried to right the plane. It was coming down in a shallow dive, coughing and spluttering all the while as if the engine might pack up at any moment. Even at that height they could see the contorted look on the pilot's face as he fought to regain control. That wasn't to be. The engine fluttered one more time and then cut out altogether. In the cockpit the pilot threw his hands in front of his face as if in absolute despair. Or perhaps he was trying to protect himself in the crash that was inevitable now.

'He's had it,' the Wizard cried. 'He's coming down in the drink.'

For a moment, as the pilot, jerking frantically at the joystick, managed to bring the seaplane's nose up, it looked as if the Wizard was going to be proved wrong. But only for a moment. Next instant, just as they started to become aware of the roar of a high-speed motor heading their way fast, the pilot lost control totally. The seaplane slammed into the water at 100 m.p.h. The impact forced the plane round dramatically. Its right wing came off with a rending of torn metal and fell to the wild white water like a great leaf. Up went its tail, and for a second the bemused spectators thought it was going to take its death plunge there and then. *Splash!* the tail slapped into the boiling sea once more and the engine cut out for good.

For what seemed a long time there was a heavy silence, broken only by the roar of the high-speed motor and the water boiling noisily from the heat of the plane. It was as if the men of the COPP couldn't quite believe that they had brought the giant plane down with a single burst of machine-gun fire: a kind of David and Goliath situation. Then the Wizard woke to their danger as some two hundred yards away the sub came into view, its crew already manning the for' ard gun under the conning tower as if they were expecting trouble, which the Wizard knew they'd get if they didn't move fast. 'Make the rendezvous,' he shouted. 'Come on, get the lead out of your arse. *Move it!*'

His cry alerted them to their danger. They started to 'move it' with renewed energy, for they guessed the launch, or whatever the German craft was, would make its appearance at any moment and then all hell would be let loose. But there was another danger-ous complication too. The Wizard saw the problem immediately, as the wounded pilot clambered out of his cockpit, waving a white scarf and crying a little weakly, *'Kamerad.'*

'Bugger it,' the Wizard cursed to no one in particular. 'The Jerries want to surrender.'

His mind raced electrically. There was no time to take them on board the sub, once it closed with the canoes and the shotdown seaplane. By then the launch would be in sight and he guessed what would happen as soon as she did. There'd be a ding-dong fight, or at the worst they would have to abandon their canoes and the Jerries would have the evidence they needed. The Tommies were recceing this stretch of the Normandy coast and they had only one reason for doing that: this was where they were going to invade. The whole success of an operation which had been in the planning for years would be in jeopardy. What in hell's name was he going to do? The Wizard made a snap decision. 'Kill them!' he yelled as the submarine at last came into view. 'Kill the whole bloody bunch of them!'

The two Scots raised their tommy guns immediately; they were the types who never questioned orders from a superior officer. Ferguson hesitated. 'But why—' he commenced, and then he realized why. He shouted to a shocked and apparently immobile Seagram, 'Come on, Charlie! You heard the Wizard!' Without appearing to take aim, he ripped off a burst from the hip.

The pilot shrieked as what appeared to be a line of red buttonholes suddenly were stitched across his chest. He stared down at them in amazement, as if he couldn't believe that this was happening to him. Then his knees crumpled. He raised his unwounded hand with the white scarf. *'Kamer—'* Next moment he went over the side with a splash.

Now Seagram joined in, feeling sick and weak, as the tommy gun rattled at his hip. This was a terrible thing they were doing. It was against all the rules of sea warfare. But it had to be done. Around in the bobbing and swaying canoes, the others were carried away by the crazy blood lust of battle and violent death. They riddled the whole fabric of the seaplane. A crew member attempted to crawl out of a rear hatch and escape into the water. He didn't get far. A horrified Seagram watched as his own bullets stitched the length of fuselage and slammed into the escaper's back. He threw up his arms, as if appealing to some god on high for mercy. But God was looking the other way this dawn. There was no mercy. He slumped half out of the hatch, his life blood streaming down the side of the bullet-riddled holes.

Then the Wizard threw his grenade. It exploded right into the wrecked plane, which was already half submerged in the sea. It exploded in a brilliant ball of red flash, which blinded the killers and brought the firing to an end. But there was no need for further firing. The seaplane was sinking rapidly now. Even as the first ratings were leaning out on the casing to grab the canoes, it had already virtually disappeared beneath the sea in a flurry of white water. Five minutes later the submarine had submerged, while above them the skipper of the German E-boat stared in bewilderment at the bits and pieces of wreckage and the body of the bullet-riddled pilot, wondering who in the devils' name had managed to do this...

Six

As April 1944 gave way to May, the entire southern half of England from the Wash to Land's End was turned into one great army camp. It was swamped with Allied soldiers of a dozen different nationalities. Even little Luxembourg, which before the war had fielded an army of exactly fifty men and had been forced to dress its firemen up as soldiers in order to make up enough for a parade, fielded its own companies of paras and artillery.

Already all movement, communications and mail had been placed under the strictest controls and censorship. In April all military leave had been cancelled. Anyone spotted in khaki outside the concentration areas – 'cages', the soldiers called them – was automatically assumed by the Red Caps, the military police, to be a deserter. That same month all diplomatic mail was ordered to be delayed and every foreign embassy in London, friendly or otherwise, was placed under police surveillance. A little later the ferry service between Britain and Eire was suspended. The authorities were not chancing any undercover member of the IRA (the country was filled with Irish labourers) betraying the great secret to the enemy. Bit by bit the island was sealed off from the outside world. The momentous day was approaching ever more rapidly.

By the middle of May 1944, the roads of rural southern England were crowded with seemingly endless convoys of trucks, tanks, artillery trailers, all rolling purposefully to the coast and what awaited them beyond. The houses bordering them shook and trembled to the roar of motors day and night.

Old ladies tied up their cats and dogs in case they got run over by the relentless stream of khaki-painted vehicles. Teachers in schools near the southern routes gave over attempting to teach; the noise was just too deafening. At night men and women tossed and turned, unable to sleep in their blacked-out bedrooms. Employers were forced to add an extra fifteen minutes to the lunch break in their workers' ten-and twelve-hour day so that they could dodge the one-way system that the Yanks had introduced to their part of the pre-Invasion staging areas.

Here the roads were policed by angry, red-faced 'snowdrops', or military policemen, carrying pistols slung at their hips – and looking as if they might use them, too. In their area, 'American-occupied England', as the locals called it in Devon, Dorset and Cornwall, the American soldiers checked and controlled the civilians as if they really were an occupying power.

Not that the young men already locked in their cages looked much like the soldiers of an occupying army. Indeed, they looked more like prisoners as they stared morosely through the wire fences of the cages, bearing warning notices which read DO NOT TALK TO THE TROOPS. It was almost as if they were men condemned, and it would be wiser for the civilians, who would not be crossing that stretch of water to face the unknown enemy, to have nothing to do with them.

In the last week of May, the Americans and British started to use smokescreens to hide this massive build-up from enemy reconnaissance planes. In their Nissen huts and tents, the 200,000 men of the initial assault force and the two million who would follow them counted off their last days. They read Penguin wartime specials and the US condensed books. They gambled. They slept in bunks, three-and four-tier high. They trekked over the fields to go to the thunder-boxes and crappers or to take luke-warm showers in huge, sacking screened enclosures. Here they'd squat in their hundreds, reading day-old *Stars & Stripes* and the British *Daily Mirror*, little khaki squares of lavatory paper which the British called 'army form blank' stacked in old food cans next to them. Mess hall queues stretched for hundreds of yards. Indeed, there were so many mouths to feed that the soldiers had to eat in three shifts. Lines of hungry, bored men stretched across the muddy fields day and night, twenty-four hours a day. The air was permanently spiced with the smell of frying bacon. Fifty-four thousand soldiers were employed in Hampshire and Sussex alone servicing the British and Canadian armies. Five thousand new cooks had been trained for the job. A whole Canadian Armoured Division was temporarily employed maintaining the installations.

About that time, as these thousands of scared, bored, bewildered young men of the assault formations stared out at the sea wondering what lay ahead of them on the other side of the Channel, the first ships of the great fleet which would transport them to

Normandy appeared. The storms that would plague the invasion fleet had commenced too. The grey-blue ships now began bobbing up and down at anchor on the heaving green water, while dark clouds scudded across the lowering sky. It was a scene that seemed to match the mood of the khaki-clad observers perfectly. It was sombre and guardedly apprehensive. The young men began to wrap themselves in a lonely cocoon of their own thoughts and fears. Now they had little desire to chat, or write letters to their loved ones outside this cut-off world of the cage or, indeed, to engage in any distraction from the inevitable that lay ahead...

The mood was little different at that tiny naval establishment controlled in that remote cove by the Wizard, save that he and his subordinates were still working flat out for their own role in what was to come, with the kind of freedom of movement not permitted the rest of the assault forces. The Wizard had other tasks that his men must carry out on the day. There would be X-craft, midget submarines positioned off the beaches to guide in the assault craft. On the beaches themselves there would be his 'battle-swimmers', brave young loners who would swim in from the X-craft and set up the beacons for the final assault, knowing that they were not likely to survive once the German defenders became aware of what was going on; they'd be shot down out of hand.

All the same the Wizard and Colonel Ferguson were primarily concerned with the attack on the key bunker, which might well stop the assault battalions of Montgomery's old Iron Division dead on the beach. As Ferguson explained to a still shaken Seagram in front of the new sand model of the assault beach, 'This is it, Charlie. This is what we expect you and your crew to do.'

Seagram nodded, but said nothing. Outside the Nissen hut the sky was overcast again and there was rain forecast in the Channel, but the weather, which matched Seagram's own sombre mood, didn't stop some matelot outside from singing, 'Little Miss Muffet sat on a tuffet, eating her curds and whey ... Up came a spider, sat down beside her, whipped his old bazooka out and this is what he said. "Get hold of this, bash, bash ..." '

Ferguson shook his head in mock wonder. 'Nothing seems to get our boys down, thank God,' he said, and then, as if speaking solely to himself, 'God if the poor devils only

175

knew.' He cleared his throat and was suddenly very businesslike. 'All right, Charlie, I'm sure you've guessed by now what your role in this matter is going to be.' He touched the sand model with his pointer. 'You're to take your tug, the only vessel of any size that could do it, up this channel – here – the one we recced.' He looked sharply at Seagram, as if he were checking his reaction.

Seagram's face showed nothing of his inner turmoil. That bloodthirsty massacre of the German seaplane crew still hung heavily on his conscience. More than once he had lain tossing and turning in a muck sweat in his bunk, reliving those terrible moments when he had fired at those defenceless Germans, willing to surrender but doomed because they might lead their intelligence people to the great secret of D-Day. 'Yes,' he heard himself say quite calmly. 'I think I have.'

'Good show, Charlie,' the Wizard said enthusiastically. As always when he was planning – and acting – his dreamy manner vanished and he radiated drive and determination. 'It's not going to be easy. But we've worked out the exact details, breadth, depths and all that sort of navigational stuff for you. We think you can do it.'

'Thank you,' Seagram responded, though he knew only too well that the Wizard was being encouraging. In coastal waters, due to wind and tide, such channels could change swiftly and dramatically. 'And then?'

'Then,' Ferguson took his cue swiftly, 'you take your tug, which will be lightly armoured at the bow, right up to the bunker – well, as close as you can get. Then my assault engineers – they're all trained infantrymen as well as sappers – will go into action.' Suddenly, the lean, handsome colonel looked very sombre. 'I'm reckoning with fifty per cent casualties in that first assault wave and perhaps ten to twenty per cent in the actual attack on the bunkers, once my chaps are through the minefields. It's a damnable price to pay. After all, they are young men with a life in front of them, some mother's son.'

Even the Wizard, normally an unemotional man, his mind constantly wrapped up in his devices, plans, projections and the like, was moved. He bit his bottom lip like a small child might. But outside the unknown sailor kept up his dirty ditty: 'Big balls, small balls, balls as big as yer head ... *Give 'em a twist around yer head...*' It was the old contrast of war, between life without care and sudden violent death.

Ferguson raised his voice, as if he were fighting not to give way to emotion. 'I shall lead the assault wave, of course. So, Charlie,' he forced a grin, 'if you don't want your old friend to die a hero's death, you've got to get that old tub of yours as close to the bunker as possible. Every yard you get closer, the fewer casualties my sappers will suffer. But, casualties or no casualties, *we've got to knock the bloody bunker out*. Do you understand that, Charlie?'

'Yes, I understand.' For a moment there was silence in the little Nissen hut, the armed sentry ceasing his pacing outside the locked door and the singing matelot vanished, his ditty ended. 'But you mentioned the tug will be lightly armoured, Peter. That might alter the whole business of navigating her down that channel.'

'We've gone into it, Charlie,' the Wizard responded swiftly. 'We checked what they did in France in '42. You remember perhaps?'

Seagram nodded. The Wizard was referring to the great commando raid on St Nazaire of that year.

The planners then were worried about the draft of the attack vessel, especially as it had to rush the lock gates in shallow water at great speed. So they avoided ballast and covered the deck to for' ard with light armour, the bridge too, not attempting to protect the engines and just hoping they wouldn't be hit. It had worked.

Ferguson saw the look of doubt on the younger man's face. Hurriedly he said, 'It's a chance we've got to take, Charlie. I and my soldiers are prepared to take it. You must, too.' It wasn't a suggestion. It was an order. Seagram realized that.

'Yessir,' he said formally, forgetting momentarily their first name basis. 'I understand. Just wanted to know where I am.'

'Of course, Charlie,' the Wizard butted in hurriedly. 'We understand your position. We are all concerned about the fate of the men under our command. But whatever losses we might incur, they will be trivial – I hope – in comparison with those the assault infantry will suffer if we don't knock out that bloody bunker.' He relaxed a little.

'I'm going to leave you, Peter, and Charlie here to work out the fine details. Then I suggest you take the afternoon off and take your minds off our problems.' He looked at the locked door, as if he half expected some enemy agent to be lurking behind it, and lowered his voice. 'It'll be the last time you'll get a break for a long while, I guess. We've got a hard-and-fast date, you see.'

The other two edged closer as the Wizard lowered his voice even further. 'It's going to be Monday.'

'The fifth of June?' Ferguson queried eagerly.

'Yes, the fifth of June. I suspect it'll be a date that will go down in history.'

'Perhaps,' Ferguson agreed and frowned. 'I wonder if we'll live to find out.'

'Of course, you will, Peter. Don't be a gloom merchant. In years to come when you're a grandpa, Peter, and your wet-bottomed offspring ask you about the fifth, you'll be able to boast, "On that Monday, children, I helped to win the war." Now what do you say to that, Peter?'

'Not much,' Ferguson answered dourly.

It was the same feeling that Seagram was experiencing at that moment: a dour sense of unreality, even other worldliness, as if all this was not happening or, if it was, he was not really part of it. For a moment or two, the two officers stood there, watching in silence as the Wizard unlocked the door, called to the armed sentry that he was coming out and then bade them goodbye.

Ferguson turned back to the sand table. 'All right, Charlie, let's get on with it, eh.'

'Yes, let's get on with it,' Seagram echoed.

Without enthusiasm they got back to work...

Seven

Again she caught him completely off guard.

He was marching down the clifftop road, with the dark clouds scudding madly across the seascape, threatening more rain, when there she was behind him again, ringing her bell and crying, as she braked her ancient Hercules bike, 'Want a ride, sailor?'

He turned, startled, and was abruptly happy, his sombre mood vanishing completely. It was the girl from the Sally Ann, flushed and pretty, her cheap summer frock blown by the wind almost up to her thighs. But if she realized she was displaying most of her delectable legs, she did not show it. Indeed, she seemed very pleased to see him again. He was, too, to see her. Suddenly her name and role came flashing into his mind, and with more lightness and lack of care than he had felt ever since the seaplane incident, he cried back, 'Lorna of the flute!'

'Trombone,' she corrected him, making a pumping gesture back and forth, as if she were playing that instrument. 'Things have moved on since I last saw you. Two of the silver band have been called up. The Royal Marines, would you believe it?' She laughed and he laughed with her. 'The bandmaster's going out of his mind. What's the band coming to and all that. Yes, we weak females are definitely taking over now. Things'll be different after the war.' Her smile vanished. It was as if the mention of the war spoiled everything. Hastily she asked, 'Where have you been? I've cycled by the camp thousands of times since I last saw you. My dad, you know, the home guard, is convinced I've got a fancy man in there behind the barbed wire.' She stopped and frowned hard as if she had just thought of something unpleasant.

'I'm flattered. I've been on a course,' he lied glibly.

'You sailors always say things like that. Women in every port.'

'How do you know? You play the fl— excuse me, trombone in the Sally Ann band.

You're supposed to be a good girl.'

She flushed momentarily and lowered her beautiful blue eyes, then she raised her gaze once more and said, almost challengingly, 'Even Sally Ann girls know just how naughty sailors are. Besides my dad's always warning me against them. They're out for only one thing.'

'Yes,' he heard himself agreeing, with surprising boldness for him, 'that's true. In the case of this particular lecherous sailor, he wants to invite you to have tea with him.'

She gave a little courtsey. 'How gallant! And this particular Sally Ann accepts the invitation gratefully and with pleasure.' She hesitated. 'Though, if you don't mind, not tea. I seem to pour millions of cups of the stuff every time I'm on duty.'

'Anything you desire.'

'What about the pub in the village? I've only been in it once actually, in the back passage where all the old ladies and gaffers sit – until my dad chased me out with his rifle.'

Somehow Seagram had the impression that all was not well in the Sally Ann girl's household, but he didn't remark on it. Instead, he responded in this new gallant fashion of his, 'The pub of your choice,

183

young damsel, it shall be.'

She smiled more prettily than ever. 'Your coach is ready for you, sir, would you like to mount it?'

'Sir would – greatly.' Once more he squeezed on to the pillion seat of the old pre-war bike. Again she ordered him to hold tight, and this time he wasn't so hesitant about placing his hands around her neat waist and feeling her body warmth. Momentarily he felt a sense of sexual excitement, then he controlled himself, knowing that despite her mock-provocative manner she was an innocent, and besides, what was the use of trying to establish a relationship, sexual or otherwise with her? Within the week he might be dead...

He had ordered a gin, God knows why. Later he told himself he had probably had some mad desire to get her drunk and try to seduce her. But when he had asked the old boy behind the smelly sixteenth-century bar for a lemonade for himself, to be told there wasn't any and he'd have to do with a glass of weak cider, she said she'd have a shandy, a small one. Yet even the shandy seemed to have its effect. She talked more than ever, waved her hands almost like a foreigner and laughed a lot. He didn't mind. It was fun being with her. A couple of times her hands came in contact with him and he felt a shiver of excitement, which he knew he should repress but couldn't.

She had had another shandy and he had longed for something stronger than the cider so that he could overcome his inhibitions, for he was drawn to her flushed excited face with a kind of almost painful yearning; yet at the same time he was moved by her – her chat about her job in the local factory; the gossip of the married women whose men were overseas but were 'carrying on' with the Yanks; the way her father dominated her life, even to the extent of coming to the factory to collect her when her shift was over. 'Once he came in full uniform with his rifle slung over his shoulder, and next morning all the girls made fun of me, saying I must be a naughty girl if my old man had to come and collect me with his gun.'

After the second cider had loosened him up a bit, he was still impressed by her innocence and childlike babble, saying the first things that came into her head. He told himself he shouldn't take advantage of her, but he was now sure it was a foregone conclusion that he would. His year-long deep hunger for a woman whom he could call his own, the knowledge that he would soon be facing almost certain death across the Channel, the finality of it all, would, he knew, triumph over his scruples.

When they had left the ancient rural pub it had still been light and the local curfew had not yet come into force. Outside she had blinked a little in the bright light of the setting sun and then said, perhaps worried what people might say, 'Would you like to walk me home ... We could go by the back lanes. We wouldn't bump into anyone I know there.' She had smiled at him in a flushed mixture of innocence and youthful desire.

He had known then that he should have made some excuse and gone back to the camp. Instead, he had decided to compromise, even to experiment in a way: kiss her a bit and perhaps feel her breasts, and then leave it to Nature to make the decision. If anything came of it, all right; if nothing did, that was all right too. He had told himself that he was leaving himself some sort of free choice.

So, with him pushing the cycle, they had walked down the narrow lanes already smelling of the summer to come, the fields glistening still with the rain of the afternoon.

All was silent. Even the thunder of the bombers which routinely crossed the coast at this point on their way to pulverize the German cities was absent. The war had vanished, but even as he had felt for and taken her hot sticky little hand, surprisingly soft for a factory girl, he knew that the war never disappeared; he and millions of young men like him carried it with them everywhere they went.

They had come to a stile and she had stood astride it while he had held up the old bike with its patched tyres and rusty spokes. She had kept her legs spread, and in the faint breeze which had whipped up the back of her skimpy frock he had seen her knickers, white cotton and patched like those a child might wear. He had felt a quickening of his heartbeat. He had placed his hand on her bottom as if giving her support, but animated by an overwhelming desire, in reality, to touch her young body. She had not drawn away. Instead it was as if she pressed her flesh more strongly into his damp hands as a sign of her acquiescence. He had been flooded with an overpowering feeling, and when she had clambered to the other side of the fence, he had taken her into his arms and kissed her with all the fullness of his heart and body. She had not resisted...

The whole affair had blown up on the same morning that Montgomery visited the remote coastal camp to thank and inspect the secret COPP. He came in his old pre-war Rolls Royce, flanked by a couple of outriders and followed by a jeep containing three military policemen. For a general who was to command the whole Invasion operation, temporarily in charge of two and a half million Allied soldiers, he appeared to make little fuss. He eyed the guard of honour, all white blanco and gleaming equipment, who welcomed him at the gate, with a casual look, gave them an equally casual salute and then entered. Here he shook the Wizard by the hand, and without bothering to survey the parade of soldiers, marines and sailors drawn up for his inspection he clambered on to the bonnet of the jeep and snapped in that incisive high-pitched voice of his, 'Break ranks and gather round, please.'

'You heard him,' the chief petty officer at the back of the men growled. 'Break frigging ranks.'

They did so, without any of the good-natured shoving and pushing of other formations ordered to do the same thing by

Montgomery. For these men were more mature than most, and most of them didn't hold out much hope of surviving what was to come. Whatever Montgomery said now would be of little importance or interest to them – they wouldn't survive to tell their nearest and dearest what the great man had said – but they were polite and so they stared up at him as he stood there in his battledress blouse and shabby civilian trousers and carrying a green gamp because there were storms in the Channel yet again and rain was forecast.

He let them wait. It was part of Montgomery's technique, just as the speech, the same one he made to all his troops, was. Unlike the politicians who toured the camps at the same time, he made no mention of the eternal verities. No mention of England. No hate. No question of revenge. Courage, freedom, liberty, the claptrap of the time didn't find a place in Montgomery's speech. It was simple. 'The German is a fine soldier ... When I look round here today, however, I see some of the finest soldiers I've ever seen in my career ... You and I have got to do a job soon ... If we have confidence in each other, we will do it ... Now that I have seen you, I have complete, utter confidence in

189

you.' He paused and gazed at their faces as if trying to etch each and every one of them on his mind's eye. The troops shuffled uncertainly. Was this the end of Montgomery's speech? It was. At the back, the old red-faced CPO reacted first. 'Three cheers for the general,' he barked in a voice tempered by years of cheap rum and even cheaper beer. 'Hip hip – *Hurrah!*'

Politely, as if they were doing him a favour, honouring his age and years of military service, they cheered. *'Hurrah ... hurrah ... hurrah!'* Some of the younger and older officers took off their caps and waved them above their heads in the traditional manner. But not many. Their minds were full of their lone suicidal missions scheduled for fifth June. General Bernard Law Montgomery was just a passing phase of these last days like a 'gash' fried egg or the fleeting glimpse of one of the Wrens' naked thighs above the black silk stocking.

The Wizard waited till the general had left before calling the parade to attention once more and then standing the men at ease to announce, 'Well, chaps, we've got three days left. We shall be leaving the camp in small groups from twenty hundred hours onwards tonight.'

Now the troops' faces were really animated. This was news, different from the General's speech. But that was perhaps the reason why he had come to talk to them in the first place: it was Montgomery's indirect way of thanking them, for unlike the assault troops, who would embark their craft in companies and battalions with scores and hundreds of their comrades, these men would steal away from England like thieves in the night, lone individuals or a couple of mates together at the most.

'We shan't use the local station,' the Wizard continued. 'That'd be a dead give-away to any spy. We'll use our own transport to get to the craft. There's a storm forecast, so watch out, don't eat too many of those fried eggs that the cooks are preparing for tonight, and those of you who are to man the X-craft, well, I suggest you don't eat too many of those baked beans.' He grinned and the men laughed. They knew what he meant. The air was foul enough in the tight confines of the midget submarines. It would certainly be fouler if anyone who ate a plateful of the 'cowboy beans' started breaking wind throughout the long wait before the first craft of the great invasion fleet hove into sight.

With that the Wizard dismissed the men to their various duties, indicating to Ferguson before he set about his own manifold tasks that he should make his arrangements with Seagram about getting his sappers to the battered old tug. Ferguson, however, didn't get far with his briefing. Together they walked the compound (for Ferguson was taking the greatest security precautions now, and he reasoned if they walked in the open, no one could overhear them), heads bowed against the steadily increasing wind coming from the sea.

He was saying, 'We should be OK, once we get 'em into the mincing machine,' by which he meant the ships' marshalling area. 'There'll be hundreds of ships' crews there, not only naval ones, but "brown jobs", as you call 'em, Charlie. My sappers won't stick out as anything strange,' when his discourse was interrupted by a shout, followed by a sharp command to 'Hold it there, or I'll fire!'

'What the deuce—' Ferguson began, startled, as an old man in Home Guard uniform, a rifle slung over his shoulder was grabbed by the sergeant of the guard, red-faced with anger.

'Let me go, you big bastard!' the old man

was crying angrily. 'I'm going to shoot him … I'm going to shoot him!'

Ferguson held up his hand for peace and nodded to the sergeant to let go of the runtish home guard, the front of his uniform wet and stinking of beer, as though he had been drinking a lot before he had plucked up enough courage to attempt to break into the little camp. 'Now then, Corporal, what's all this about?' he asked in the manner of an officer who was used to handling the complaints of silly drunken soldiers.

'It's him,' the home guard spluttered. 'Him there in naval uniform.' He indicated a suddenly scarlet-faced Seagram. 'That sex fiend there. He's gone and ruined my lass, the swine.'

'Ruined,' Ferguson commenced in his urbane manner. 'What do you mean?'

'This.' With his free hand, the home guard pulled out a pair of knickers from inside his open, stained battledress blouse.

With an abrupt sinking feeling, Seagram recognized the knickers. They were the ones that the Sally Ann girl had worn when he had helped her over the stile.

The man opened up the pants to display the bloodstain in the crotch of the poor, darned clothing. 'He did that to her. Young lass of eighteen. Took her virginity away without even a promise of marriage. Sex fiend, that's what the bastard is. For all I know he raped her, though she sez he didn't—'

'All right, all right.' Ferguson held up his hands for peace. 'That's enough. What do you want us to do?'

'*You? Me!*' I'm gonna shoot the bugger!'

'No, you're not.' Now Ferguson had had enough. 'You're going to leave here peacefully, or I'm going to have my sergeant deal with you. And he's not the peaceful type.'

The sergeant of the guard, who seemed to know the drunken Home Guard corporal, beamed suddenly and said, 'With your permission, sir, it'd give me the greatest of pleasure.'

Ferguson didn't seem to hear. Instead, he said, 'If you've got a complaint against any of my people, then you must go to the civil police. It's their duty to deal with such matters. Is that clear?'

The Sally Ann girl's father gave Ferguson a sullen look and opened his mouth as if he were going to say more, but then he saw that the sergeant had clenched his fists, which were like small steam shovels, and decided he'd better not. Instead, he changed his Ross rifle from one skinny shoulder to the other and moved away, but when he came to where the road turned into the little camp, he called, 'Don't think I'm afraid of you. You'll be hearing from me again, mark my words.'

'Frig off, while you still can,' the big sergeant of the guard growled, and took one step forward threateningly.

Hastily the old man retreated, still mumbling to himself. Ferguson relaxed a little. Turning to a crimson-faced, completely embarrassed Seagram, who was staring down at the bloodstained, patched knickers which the home guard had dropped in his haste to get away from the big sergeant, he said quietly, 'Don't worry about it, Charlie. We've got bigger, much bigger, problems ahead of us in the next few days. Personal problems don't exist any more.' He added the words as if he were trying to convince himself of the truth of that observation. Then, touching his cap casually, he walked off, suddenly deep in thought.

The sergeant of the guard waited till Colonel Ferguson had gone, before picking up the soiled pants and saying, 'Do you want me to get rid of them for you sir? They're not much cop as they are.'

Numbly Seagram nodded, his mind totally blank.

The NCO stuffed the knickers in his battledress pocket. Lowering his voice, he said, 'I wouldn't take much notice of the silly old fart, sir, if I was you. They say in the village pub that he's after half the young lasses in the village. Real young ' uns at that, if you take my meaning, sir.' He looked significantly at the young officer. 'They're all alike these frigging Holy Joes, going to frigging church every frigging Sunday that frigging dawns. As my old ma used to say o' that kind, they talks water and drinks wine.' He frowned and looked hard at Seagram. 'All right, sir?'

Seagram shook his head like a man attempting to awake from a bad dream. 'Yes thanks, Sergeant, I'm fine.'

'Then that's OK, sir.' He pulled himself to attention and flung Seagram a tremendous salute. Then he marched smartly back to the guardroom, bloodstained knickers dangling from his pocket, leaving Seagram alone with his thoughts. They weren't very pleasant. Half an hour later, Charlie Seagram was quite drunk.

Eight

On the evening of 2nd June, 1944, the first of the Wizard's COPP advance forces slipped out of Portsmouth's East Gate. As darkness started to close around the two midget submarines, they steamed to their rendezvous. They were to meet a group of trawlers and the craft that would protect them, a number of ML escorts. They surfaced east of Spithead, where the trawlers were waiting for them. The sea was rough for the midget subs, but somehow the trawlermen managed to get their tow fixed between themselves and the X-craft, and within half an hour they were on their way, with the trawlers heading for France pulling the midget subs on their stern. The secret operation was on its way, just three days short of the great invasion, which would commence the following Monday.

At dawn, the towing craft and the two subs parted company. 'G-O-O-D L-U-C-K', the trawlers signalled discreetly, and vanished into the darkness. The handful of COPP crewmen were alone in their cramped quarters, where even the smallest of them couldn't stand upright and they could turn only with difficulty, due to the instruments and signal equipment which was packed everywhere. As the bleak wet dawn grew lighter, the subs headed south together, the crews eating their breakfast: thick chunks of bread and butter, followed by ration chocolate and boiled sweets. Cooking was virtually impossible, it ate up too much air.

About mid-morning, the vanguard parted and both subs headed on individual courses for the French coast. Some time later, the *X-23* dived and then rose to periscope height cautiously. For now extreme care was needed. Not only would their own lives be forfeited if they were discovered by the enemy, but perhaps the success of the whole great landing operation. Sweating hard the sub commander searched the coast through the corrugated glass of the scope. It seemed deserted: a barren wasteland of tidal flats and dunes. Then the sub commander had it. It was the Ouistreham Light. Now he went to work with renewed energy. He was roughly in the right spot. Taking a dozen or so cross-bearings, he estimated that he was now in position west of the River Orne.

There the paras of the 6th Airborne would land and the left flank of the Iron Division's assault would go in. He'd even spotted the key stream, which the Wizard had emphasized he had to find and pinpoint. It was vital.

For a moment the skipper of the X-craft relaxed. It was Sunday. Over on the land the pious Norman peasants would be soon going to their churches, followed by a gossipy session in the local *estaminets* and *bistros*, drinking their cider and calvados before going home to a heavy lunch and a snooze with the old woman afterwards. The skipper grinned. He wouldn't mind at this minute being home in bed with the old woman – anybody's old woman for that matter. Then the signaller behind him murmured, 'Watch it, sir. I'm gonna let one rip.' He did and the tight casing was filled with the stink of methane gas.

'Dirty sod,' the skipper muttered routinely, and then forgot his carnal thoughts to remember the other young men on the English side of the narrow sea. In twenty-four hours, if the weather didn't get worse, the vast fleet now massed along the south-east coast of Britain would sail. Many of the young men on board those ships would die this coming week. In front of him the length of the French coast would erupt in a mass fury of shells and bombs. There, too, not only young German men would die, but also civilians, men, women and children. It seemed totally unreal, but it would happen. The skipper sighed. Now there was nothing for him and his crew to do but wait here at the bottom of the sea, play cards and doze and listen for the signal which would order them to light their lamps and give welcome to the invading fleet. Behind him the sailor who had farted started to sing softly, 'Tight as a drum, never been done. Queen of all the fairies. Isn't it a pity she's only one titty to feed the baby on...'

The skipper grinned. It was not exactly the Battle Hymn of the Republic but it seemed an apt enough song to go into battle in this crazy war. He closed his eyes and started to dream of nubile, naked young women...

The Wizard, more worried than he had ever been before a landing, and he had taken part in landings in North Africa, Sicily, Greece and Italy, listened to the usual statistics coming across the Tannoy system for the sake of the soldiers and sailors waiting everywhere. 'There will be two task forces, known as the western and eastern task

200

forces. Each task force will consist of an assault force, a follow up one, a bombarding one and several minesweeping flotillas. Each of these two task forces, one commanded by Rear Admiral Kirk of the US Navy, the other by Rear Admiral Sir Philip Vian of the Royal Navy, will be completely self-sufficient. The warships and larger vessels involved will be seventy-five per cent British and twenty-five per cent American.' That caused cheers from the British and boos from the Americans present. On any other occasion, the Wizard would have smiled, but not now. He was too worried.

'It is estimated that the total number of ships and craft involved in these first assault waves will number four thousand vessels, a figure which does not include the hundreds of smaller craft being carried to the invasion beaches by other vessels ... Over eighty ships will take part in the initial bombardment. Equipped with six hundred guns from four-inch calibre to sixteen-inch, they will bring down two thousand tons of high explosive in the first ten minutes of the attack...'

For a moment the Wizard forgot the statistics meant to cheer up the men who would carry out the actual assault, and stared out at the crowded seascape, with the white-capped heaving sea beyond. The weather was getting worse by the hour, he could see that. The question now was were the powers-that-be going to be able to commence the great operation on 5th June, as planned. If they weren't, what was he to do with his men? Not only did he have his X-craft out there off the French coast, but also his battle swimmers and the COPP guides who were due to sail at any moment with the swimming tanks of the 13th/18th Hussars, guiding them to the spots where they would land in front of the assault infantry and tackle the German bunkers. How could his men and special craft stand yet more time at sea just off the French coast without being discovered by the Germans or drowned by the ever mounting raging seas? It was a damnable problem for a commander who was devoted to his men but who had also put his life's blood into making this operation a success. What the hell was he to do?

While the Wizard waited for the vital information that might occasion him to stand his men down till the storms had abated, Colonel Ferguson was facing his own problems. His men, all bronzed veterans of operations in the Middle East, were not a real source of trouble, though some of them seemed to start retching miserably and being sick immediately they stepped on the deck of Seagram's shabby rusty old tub. Admittedly, even in the quieter water of Southampton Docks, she was a bit of a nuisance. The extra frontal armour which was to protect her bow and bridge made the old ship unwieldy, and she tossed about as if she were at sea, not securely anchored among scores of other small craft bound for France and the great attack.

His problem was Seagram.

The young officer had been drinking solidly ever since the confrontation with the Home Guard corporal. At first, after he had really got sozzled, he had tried to hide his drinking from Ferguson. But it hadn't worked. Now it was commonplace to see him working a zigzag course to the great open officers' mess and try to buy whisky, gin, rum, anything alcoholic from fellow officers who didn't drink – and he was prepared to pay any price for a bottle. Ferguson guessed he must have already forfeited his pay for a couple of months to come to pay for his booze.

Of course, the simplest course would have been to dismiss him from his ship: the

Wizard, with his clout, could have managed that easily and without any scandal. But what then? Ferguson knew that it would have been virtually impossible to replace Seagram with a skipper who knew the crew, the old tub and the mission as Seagram did at such short notice. At the same time, how could he rely on a drunken Seagram carrying out his all-important mission in the state he was currently in?

Although he was rushed off his feet ensuring that his assault engineers had every conceivable piece of equipment they might possibly need when – and if – they got close enough to the damned hidden bunker to knock it out, the Seagram problem was with him all the time. A couple of times he had tried to approach the younger officer in an attempt to discuss the business of the Sally Ann girl with him. But Seagram had refused to be drawn on both occasions, and Ferguson had realized after the second attempt that any mention of the problem only seemed to make Seagram drink more. Now he was back to where he had been when Admiral Challenger had first introduced him to Seagram. The pocket of his tunic bulged again with his silver hip flask, and when he thought he wasn't being observed

Seagram would whip it out and take a hefty drink of whatever damned alcohol it contained.

But Ferguson's anger at Seagram's behaviour was also tempered by a certain compassion. He could understand Seagram's reasons for succumbing again to drink. During the last terrible years of war he had met many officers like Charlie. The strain had been just too much for them. A few had cracked up altogether and had been sent to the funny farm, or they had been cashiered, reduced to the ranks, and been posted to the 'shit-shovellers', the Pioneer Corps. Most of them had soldiered on, just like Seagram, attempting to continue to do their duty despite the stress and strain. All the same, they needed alcohol to keep them going – and alcohol and combat didn't go well together. The Seagrams of this world, he told himself, had to be pitied and understood. Yet at the same time they presented a danger. How good was their judgement in a moment of crisis? Would they need that extra buzz of alcohol which they felt would keep them going, but which, by the same token, could often slow their reaction time, their ability to make the swift correct decision on which the success of an operation depended?

'Christ Almighty!' he cursed to himself more than once that long day, while the Wizard and many others waited for the order to go. 'I'd bloody well like to go and get drunk out of my mind myself.' But Colonel Ferguson knew he'd never do that. Cynical he may have become about the war and what would come in the peace that would follow, once they'd won it, but he realized where his duty lay.

On that particular afternoon, with the wind rising ever more steadily, darker and darker clouds scudding across the Channel, the Wizard returned, his thin face as gloomy as the weather. 'It's bloody well off,' he announced in disgust. He flung his battered old cap on the table angrily.

'You mean the invasion? How long?'

'At least twenty-four hours. The bigshots down at Pompey – Eisenhower, Monty and the rest – have decided we can't risk it in such weather conditions. So they've postponed it in the hope that on the sixth the weather will be better.'

Ferguson sucked his teeth and whispered, 'Bollocks!'

'Bollocks indeed. Think of my poor chaps over there being told they've got to risk another twenty-four bloody hours sitting right under the Hun's big noses. It's enough to drive even the toughest of them up the wall.'

'They'll stick it out,' Ferguson encouraged him.

'Yes, of course they will. They're a good bunch of fellows. They know what's expected of them. Some of them have risked their lives time and time again.' He forgot his X-crews and the lone battle-swimmers already in position on the other side of the Channel and asked, 'What of young Charlie? Is his mood any better?'

Ferguson shook his head. ' 'Fraid not. That business with the Sally Ann girl and her father still weighs heavily on him. He simply can't stop drinking. He's capable, but only just.'

'Can you do anything about him?'

'I've tried, but he won't listen or he avoids me.' Ferguson frowned deeply. 'I don't know—'

'Can he carry out the job?' the Wizard asked, and there was iron in his voice now. 'Or will the booze get to him?'

'Frankly I don't know. A week or so ago I would have laid my arm in the fire for him. He was a reformed character. He felt respected and had been given an important job to do. Now...' Ferguson shrugged and left the rest of his sentence unspoken.

The Wizard pondered his answer for a few moments. Outside, officers, looking tired and worn, were drifting back slowly to their billets. They, too, had just learned the news that D-Day had been postponed to the following Tuesday. Now they'd have to get themselves worked up to face the strain and stress of the new date on the morrow. All of them looked as if they'd had enough, couldn't go on much longer like this. Watching them, the Wizard told himself that he couldn't allow his own little command to be subjected to too much of this kind of thing any longer. He made his decision. 'All right, Peter, this is what I think you should do.'

'Go on,' Ferguson responded eagerly, clutching at straws.

'I know I can't really expect a colonel of engineers to get mixed up in these domestic matters – star-crossed lovers and all that bullshit. But what we have planned for young Charlie is more important than that. So I'm asking you if you would buzz over to the village and see if you can talk to the girl from the Salvation Army and get her to send young Charlie something, perhaps a little letter, which will perk him up ... something that'll stop him boozing like this and give him a clear head and a steady hand on the morrow.'

Ferguson looked uncertain and the Wizard went on hurriedly, 'Remember this great undertaking we are engaged in, Peter. I hate to sound so bloody formal, almost Churchillian, but that's what it is, and we are duty bound to see that it succeeds. There's a buckshee motorbike behind my billet. I'll sign the ticket for the petrol for it. Hell, Peter, I'll sign it 'the Supreme Commander', if you wish, and risk a couple of years in the clink for doing so. But I beg you, go and try your best.' He placed his hands together in mock supplication.

Ferguson gave him a weary smile. 'All right, old lad, I'll have a bash, but I can't promise—'

'Of course you can't. Just go.'

Ferguson went.

Nine

Ferguson skidded to a stop in front of the great factory just as the place's whistles and sirens started to sound the end of the second shift of the day. He lifted his goggles and slapped the dust from his uniform, peering red eyed at the shabby crowd of women and older men streaming out of the plant on foot or on their bikes. At the gate the security man nodded and then pointed to a slim girl on her own, who, hanging back from the rest, was tying up her head scarf, as if she didn't want to be with the rest of the crowd.

Ferguson thought he would feel the same in her position. They did look a poor under-nourished lot with their skinny bodies, shabby old clothes and pale faces. The war had taken its toll, he told himself. These people had suffered and worked damned hard over the last five years. It didn't take a crystal ball to see that they were about at the end of their tether. The war would have to come to a conclusion soon, or else.

Then he dismissed the shabby crowd of

workers and concentrated on the girl, edging himself and his Norton closer to where she would come through the gates. He had already been told by the factory's security over the phone that the Sally Ann girl's father often came to pick her up – 'And anything else in a short skirt that he can pick up, too, the dirty old bugger' – at the end of her shift. Ferguson wanted to get her away before that eventuality arose.

Now she was level with him. Seagram had described her as 'happy and red cheeked, Ferguson, you know, the English rose type.' Now there was nothing of the English rose about Miss Lorna Hodgson. She looked pale, with dark bags under her eyes, as if she might well cry often.

'Miss Hodgson,' he called. 'Lorna Hodgson!'

She turned slowly, in no way startled at being addressed by a man in the uniform of a lieutenant colonel sitting astride a motorbike. It was almost as if she was in some kind of a daze, even a trance. 'Yes?' she answered in a weak voice.

'My name's Ferguson,' he said swiftly, spotting the Home Guard uniform some hundred or so yards away. 'I'm a friend of Lieutenant Seagram. He asked me to see you ... But hop on the bike. We can't talk here.'

Before she could object he had bundled her on to the pillion seat, shouted as she had once done to Seagram, 'Hold tight,' and had roared away at full throttle. Behind them her father stopped and shook his fist with rage. At the gate the security man grinned and said to no one in particular, 'Put that in yer pipe and smoke it, you frigging old lecher.'

Unwittingly he took her to the pub where it had all begun with Seagram. There were a couple of farm labourers drinking cider in the public bar, but the 'snug', into which he took her, still surprised and protesting, was empty save for a fairly well-dressed woman, who didn't look like a local and who was drinking an expensive gin and tonic. For a moment their eyes met, then she saw the girl and she grinned in a knowing way for a moment before turning her attention back to her drink.

Swiftly Ferguson told as much as he dared of his reason for coming here, and how Charlie was going to pieces because of her and the scene with her father, the Home Guard corporal.

What appeared to him to be a long silence followed. He was somewhat embarrassed, wondering what to say to convince her of the importance of cheering Charlie up and stopping him drinking. At the bar the woman with the gin and tonic smiled at him. He guessed she thought he, the older man and an officer at that, was trying to proposition this shabby young innocent working girl. While he waited for Lorna to say something, he sized the other woman up. She had a fleshy mobile body, not very English, more like the Eyetie women they had frequented when they had come out of the line at Salerno and Anzio. For some reason he smiled back. Perhaps he was trying to convince her that he wasn't on the make, trying to get the knickers off this innocent next to him, sipping a shandy.

The woman didn't respond immediately. Then she uncrossed her legs deliberately. He caught a glimpse of the plump white flesh above the tops of her black silk nylons. As concerned and agitated as he was, he suddenly felt excited. He realized he hadn't had a woman for months. He swallowed and nodded to the publican. 'Scotch,' he mouthed. The man pulled a face, as if it would hurt him to serve a glass of his precious whisky; then he changed his mind and brought a double across and a carafe of lukewarm water. Ferguson dropped two half-crowns on his tray and said, 'Keep the change.' The publican beamed. 'Just shout up, sir, when you need another.'

'He'll kill me, you know,' Lorna said hoarsely, completely out of the blue.

'Who?'

'My dad.'

'Why?' Ferguson heard himself say, wondering what the devil he had got himself into.

'Because he doesn't want me to have anything to do with Charlie, or any other man for that matter.' She lowered her gaze momentarily as if she was suddenly ashamed. 'He wants me for himself, you see.'

Ferguson gasped, shocked. 'For himself! What do you mean, Lorna?'

She didn't answer immediately.

Across the snug the woman was gazing at them seriously, as if she were making some sort of decision. She looked to Ferguson like a woman who had been around, but she didn't have that look of faked interest – the flash of the eyes, the inviting smile – of the whores he'd known, the only kind of woman available to a fighting soldier. Her look said: 'You're having trouble with the girl, aren't you? Anything I can do to help?'

But at that moment a shocked Ferguson couldn't think of anything the woman could do. Indeed he couldn't think of anything *he* could do; Lorna's revelation was too revolting for him to think clearly.

'He said I'd sinned in the field with Charlie,' she continued in a kind of emotionless monotone. 'I'd lost my purity. No man'd look at me again. He said I'd have to let him look after me in the future – *in that way*.'

'The perverted bastard,' Ferguson swore.

She didn't seem to hear. She said, 'Then he wanted to see what Charlie had done to me.'

'See what?'

Again she lowered her gaze and muttered, so that he had to strain to hear her. 'My thing ... He touched it ... and said that's how my mum's thing had looked when he'd first done it to her ... But they'd been married ... I wasn't. Now every man that came near would know that I was a fallen woman...' She licked her lips, dry with the effort of so much talking, and he held up her glass of cider. She took a sip and murmuring, 'Thanks,' continued. 'Then he went crackers, got out his Home Guard uniform and his rifle. He pulled my knickers from under the bed and swore he'd kill Charlie for what he'd done to me, making me into a loose woman like this.' Suddenly she laughed bitterly. 'Course he wouldn't. He's scared of his own bloody shadow. It was just to impress me, make sure that I was his woman ... He's been waiting till he could have me ever since Mum died and I became—'

'Stop,' Ferguson commanded. 'I don't want to hear any more, my dear. Your father belongs in jail. He can't get away with this kind of thing. It's against the law. He has to be stopped.'

She laughed softly in that new cynical manner she seemed to have acquired. 'Too late, sir. He has got away with it.'

'You mean?'

'The very next night ... when he came home from the pub.' Then she began to cry, her thin shoulders heaving as her skinny body was racked by sobs like a broken hearted child.

'Oh my God,' Ferguson cried. 'Oh my God, what a bloody world...'

'You married, Peter?' the woman asked and kissed him again before he could answer. They sat there on the overstuffed, creaking Victorian sofa in her high-ceilinged room, cold and uninviting, with the last few embers of coal dying in the grate.

'Was. Before I went out to North Africa in '42.'

She nodded and took a sip of her G and T.

'Been out there three months when I got a "Mespot" – "Dear John"'s the Yanks call 'em. Usual stuff. Met somebody else, wanted a divorce – that sort of thing.'

In the hall of her big gloomy house, the grandfather chimed the hour. It was the only sound, save the creaking of the wood, to break the brooding silence of the place. The two of them might well have been the last people alive in the world.

He took a drink of his whisky, her last bottle, she had said, and asked, 'You?'

'Widow of sorts. Killed at St Nazaire. So long ago now that I've almost forgotten him.' She shrugged. 'Sad. But there've been others.' She touched his glass with hers in a kind of toast. 'The war's done for people like us. That kid too.'

He nodded. She needed to put up the blackout, but somehow it didn't seem important any more. The decisions had been all made. One way or another the war had been decided. For good or bad.

'Can't do much for her really. She refuses to go to the police, as I've told you. Scandal,

I suppose. She thinks she's a fallen woman. Nothing can change that now.'

'Fallen woman,' she echoed, and snickered. 'I guess all of us of a certain age are fallen women now. Men have been away too long.'

'Do you want to do it again?' he asked, ignoring her remark, noting how the nipples of her ample breasts had become erect under the thin material of her blouse. She was either cold or excited, he concluded.

'I thought you'd never ask.' She smiled. 'You're my this night's treat. Goes with a hot bath and change of knickers.' She leaned over and kissed him on the mouth. Her lips tasted of gin.

He smiled too. 'Do you have many treats?'

'Not too often. As my local butcher – another dirty old man – used to say before he went away, "Don't give him steak every day, missus, or he'll stop appreciating it".' She mimicked the local rural accent nicely.

Ferguson knew who 'he' was – had been, he corrected himself mentally. 'Never been compared to steak before.' He put his hands on her breasts. They were firm and the nipples were very erect now. She certainly was excited. For a moment he thought of young Charlie and the girl. But only for a moment. There was nothing more he could do about them. He forgot the star-crossed lovers and squeezed her breasts cruelly. Her stomach rose into his and he felt himself grow erect. She pulled up her skirt and spread her legs once more...

Afterwards she let him doze on the sofa for another quarter of an hour. Then he had asked her to wake him. He had to get back to Southampton long before dawn; he'd be court-martialled if he didn't. She didn't ask why; it didn't interest her. She'd never see him again anyway, she knew that already. She stared at him as he lay there on the rumpled cushion, the icy silver of the moonlight illuminating his stern soldier's face. He hardly seemed to be breathing. She frowned for some reason. For all she knew, he might well be dead already...

BOOK THREE

The Day of Destiny

Our life is closed, our life begins,
The long, long anchorage we leave,
The ship is clear at last, she leaps!
She swiftly courses from the shore
Joy, shipmate, joy.

Whitman

One

Like beasts of burden, laden down with equipment and weapons, the men of Ferguson's Assault Engineers filed aboard the old tub. Each man of the assault force had a number chalked on his helmet, so that there would be no confusion over individuals and squads.

Out at sea it was still dark, but already the gulls and other scavengers wheeled and dived over the mighty fleet now beginning to depart in expectation of waste and other offerings, such as once the fishermen had thrown them. But all that the infantry of the Iron Division were depositing over the sides of their vessels was vomit, for most of them were seasick even before they had left port.

Ferguson, the veteran, watched his men with a practised eye. He noted that his assault squads were filing forward correctly. They would land in reverse order with the first wave, laden with Bangalore torpedoes, mine-detectors, flame-throwers and the like, in front. All was going perhaps too well. It had been like this at Anzio until things had started to go bloody wrong.

Ferguson forgot the Italian beachhead where the Allies had been bogged down for four long bloody months and stared at the dark sea dotted everywhere with silhouettes of hundreds of ships. The storm had begun to abate, but the men in those ships had been in the Channel for twenty-four, forty-eight hours already. He could imagine what their ships were like, awash with vomit and half-digested food, the stink nauseating, causing more sickness. Now the ships were beginning to move, and he could feel for those unknown young infantrymen who would carry the assault. Sick or not, they'd be alienated by the strange sensation of being suspended in time, crawling steadily forward through the grey waste to the unknown. It was an awesome feeling.

A flight of Spitfires zoomed in low, the roar of their engines drowning the steady thud-thud of the transports' engines. At any other time, his men would have raised their heads and cheered the RAF boys. Not now. They were too concerned with their own fates and what lay ahead of them. Someone among his troops attempted to raise the mood of his comrades with the old ditty, 'We're saying good-bye to them all ... the long and the short and the tall ... So cheer up my lads, fuck 'em all...' But the men's mood was too sombre. No one joined in. The ditty died away into nothing.

Now he turned his attention to the bay. Here the convoy had nearly formed up. Already the two Royal Navy frigates which would escort them were beginning to blow hoots on their systems, and the bosuns' whistles were signalling everywhere on deck. Between them the five-thousand-ton transports wallowed on the swell waiting to move off with their human cargoes. The tanks and the DUKWS which would carry the assault infantry of the East Yorks and the South Lancs were already loaded: twenty-odd floating tanks and four DUKWS, invariably known to the infantrymen as 'ruptured ducks'. Above, the protective barrage balloons bobbed up and down in the wind like rubber elephants. All was controlled chaos, hectic movement, angry orders, mumbled complaints combining to form one huge rolling armada setting out to the greatest invasion the world had ever known.

Despite his mood Ferguson was awed by the historic enormity of it all. There had never been a military operation of this magnitude before; there would never be another one in the future. Then he remembered the woman as he had left her on his motorbike only hours before. Suddenly, surprisingly for such an experienced woman, who had known many men in this war, she had broken down. Even as he had revved up the reluctant machine, she had cried a little drunkenly, 'Fuck off you brave officer and gentleman. Go and get yourself fucking killed!'

Caught completely off guard, he had stopped revving the Norton and turned to her. Her hair was dishevelled and one of her delightful breasts had worked itself loose from her low-cut blouse, so that it hung there in the cold moonlight like that of a loving mother offering it to some beloved babe to be suckled. 'What,' he had begun, but she had cut him off sharply: 'You've cast yourself as a bloody brave soldier who is bound to die, well fuck off and die!'

'But, darling—'

'Don't bloody darling me! Only fucking characters in fucking cheap novels are condemned to do something right from the start. There are ways out. You think there aren't because you're not bloody well thinking of yourself. You're thinking of country and King-Emperor. You don't need to die—' Abruptly she could say no more. She had hung her head as if she might break down again and sob at any moment. He reached out a hand in one last attempt to touch her, for he knew he'd never see her again, but she had shrugged him off and without looking back, head still hung sadly, she had walked back to the house in the cold light of the spectral moon and slammed the door behind her. He had started the machine and without revving the engine now – for it seemed wrong to disturb the silence of the night – he had ridden away.

Now, as Ferguson dismissed the woman whom he'd known only for a matter of hours but who had seemed to be more concerned than any of the ones he had known for months, he turned to find himself facing Seagram. As usual, he smelled of drink, but he didn't seem to be affected by it.

'Peter,' he said, 'we're ready to cast off.' He hesitated momentarily. 'I hear through the grapevine that you've been to see – er – Lorna, Peter.'

Ferguson knew who that 'grapevine' was. It was the Wizard. He was pulling out all the stops to ensure that Seagram didn't make a mess of the great attack.

'Yes, as a matter of fact, Charlie, I have.'

To their front green signal flares were hissing into the night sky. An Aldis lamp was clacking out an urgent message. Whistles shrilled. Somewhere a bunch of dockers were cheering hoarsely. The convoy was beginning to move.

'And?'

Ferguson was suddenly furious with the Wizard. The bastard was forcing his hand. He was making him lie. But there was no other way. 'Naturally I didn't have much time with her, but she said she was going to leave home – the factory will help to find a billet in the village, they've assured me. She ... she sends her love.'

Ferguson could sense rather than see that the young naval officer was not entirely convinced. Hesitantly he asked, 'Did she send me a note or anything, Peter?'

Afterwards Ferguson wondered where he had learned to lie so glibly and fast, for he answered straightaway, 'Funny you should ask that, Charlie. She was going to scribble you a note there and then, but damn if we could find a pencil and scrap of paper. So I said she should write you a proper letter as soon as she got to the new billet, with an address for you to answer to. I gave her our Field Post Office Number. 'Spect you'll get the letter with the first batch that reaches us.'

'I say, Peter,' Seagram breathed, 'that's really wonderful. I'd like to thank you—'

'Come on there, tug,' an official voice boomed through a loud-hailer across the anchorage. 'Let's get this party on the road, old chap. Or do you need a ruddy written invitation...? Move it now!'

Seagram moved it, doubling for the rusty sandbagged little bridge, while behind him Ferguson breathed a sigh of relief, telling himself what a damned fraud he really was. Slowly, as the crew cast off, the tug, its screw churning the oily water, was on its way. The stage was set, the actors were in place, the drama could commence...

Their Lordships' signal was faint. But there. Definite. The huge listening towers of the German navy's Intelligence service just outside Flensburg and Hamburg picked it up immediately. In their air-conditioned underground, bomb proof chambers, the bespectacled decoders of the night shift, German graduates of US Ivy League colleges and British Oxbridge, went to work on the signal immediately. They knew the situation in southern England. They knew the code – well almost. But they were very bright and very experienced. In just less than thirty minutes they had cracked the signal. Their senior member, who affected a languid manner and a snow-white handkerchief tucked into his sleeve in the slightly decadent English manner, gave the awkward prose of the transcript a slight polish and then sent the decode winging its way to the various German naval headquarters along the French-occupied coast.

For once the headquarters staff officers, usually so suspicious of Intelligence and the 'nervous Nellies' who worked in it, acted at once. Almost within seconds they were on the red scrambler phones alerting the E-boat bases at Le Havre and Cherbourg. The E-boat commanders at the French bases had hardly time to put their phones down when the sirens were shrieking their dire warnings the lengths of the quays against which the lean dangerous-looking craft were tied up. The pasty-faced young officers in their leather overalls snapped into action at once. Here and there as their crews tumbled out of their bunks and began putting on their uniforms frantically, the commanders ran up the black and white flag of the *Kriegs-marine*. But most of the young men who commanded the torpedo boats had very personal emblems: a broom (to sweep the seas clean); some red flannel drawers taken from some French granny; the usually black silk frilly knickers 'won' from the whores they frequented.

Naturally there was always a flotilla comedian who had to be different. Even among these young men who expected to live a short life and make a handsome corpse, there had to be one who was more outrageous than the rest. Theirs was 'Crazy Carl', a tall young man with a red, permanently dripping large nose, whose personal flag was a huge black bra taken from a Parisian whore whose breasts had been so enormous that the young sailors who had seen her 'perform' would cry, 'Tuck yer head between them milk puddings, comrades, and yer'll be deaf for weeks to come.'

But 'Crazy Carl' had naturally had to be different. Somehow he had convinced a tailor to add the third cup in the same black material. Now, as the E-boats throbbed and roared, making the light wooden craft tremble as if they might disintegrate at any moment, he hoisted his 'three tits' personal emblem, saluted it with a rigid 'Heil Hitler' and yelled at his crew, 'What better way to go to war, comrades, than under the sign of the three black tits!' He blew the battle flag a wet kiss and cried in the harsh voice of an experienced skipper, *'Leinen los!'*

On the jetty, the French workmen, one day to boast they had always been keen members of the resistance, *naturally*, let go of the ropes as the craft trembled and strained like pedigree racing dogs eager to be released from their leashes. 'Let go for'ard,' Carl the comedian cried. *'Los* ... full power!'

The lead motorboat slid away immediately, whipping the water up to a white fury with its twin screws. Carl followed. He felt the old kick in his guts as it hit the first wave. He tightened his stomach muscles automatically. Soon the battering would come which had ruined all their guts and made them white faced and sickly with permanently damaged stomachs. Their speed increased. The sluggish green of the estuary was churned a brilliant white. Then they were out of the harbour. Carl and the rest of the young captains eased their throttles open even more. The great engines howled. One by one their knife-like bows rose out of the water. They seemed to be skimming the surface of the sea. More speed. Now their prows were hitting the waves at forty knots, striking each one as if it was a brick wall. Now they were heading due west to take up the challenge. If they were sailing to meet the invasion, Davids against some modern-day Goliath, they'd stop it. In the second E-boat, just behind the flotilla leader, that monstrous three black tit emblem blossoming out fully, Carl's keen gaze darted intently from the green dials of the bridge instruments to the dark sea ahead and then from port to starboard. The hunter was intent on his prey...

Both the X-craft were shipping water now. The battering they had taken from the gales of the last forty-eight hours had taken their toll. Their pumps were working all-out to contain the water that had poured through the forehatch. Worse still, their gyro compasses had broken down so the weary crews had no means of checking their exact positions. Still, the midget submarine covering the channel that led to the hidden bunker had established that it hadn't changed its course; it was still where it was supposed to be. Patiently her skipper started to signal to seaward, using a green shade. Out there the armada was approaching. Five minutes or so later, as the horizon was tinged the faint pink of the new dawn, he ran up a flag in place of the signal. Then, straining his eyes, he could just make out the faint line of the first wave of the landing barges. They were like sea-tossed water beetles, silhouetted faintly against the breaking day. He yawned and told himself that he could sleep for ever, if he had a chance. But that wasn't to be. As yet another flight of twin-engined Mitchells came in low and started dropping their deadly eggs on the hinterland to interdict any attempt to rush up supplies and troops to the endangered beaches, he knew his day wasn't over yet. It never would be. He and his crew would be dead before this 6th June 1944 was out: forgotten heroes, like so many young men who would fight and die this Tuesday.

A couple of miles from where the two X-craft waited to guide the first assault wave in, Ferguson and Seagram tensed on the sandbagged bridge of the rusty old tug. To left and right of them there were two squadrons of the 13/18th Hussars being guided in by their comrades of the COPP. The swimming tanks had spent a terrible night. Engines had broken down, tows had parted, radios had gone crazy, charts had been drenched by wave after wave swamping them. Now, with a certain kind of relief, although so many of them were going to their deaths, they homed in on the signal from the midget sub.

Ferguson and Seagram did the same. 'So far so good, said the actress to the bishop,' Ferguson quipped. Seagram allowed himself a soft chuckle. Then he concentrated on the beach. It was just as it had been depicted on the sand tables. 'Marvellous,' he shouted against the sudden crash and thunder of the big naval guns further out to sea, as the Allied battleships commenced their bombardment, adding to the racket of the air attack. 'Exactly as we've been briefed.'

'Right!' Ferguson cupped his hands around his mouth and shouted back. 'Still haven't spotted that bloody channel yet, though.'

'We will do soon,' Seagram shouted back, full of the new confidence that the promise of a letter from Lorna had occasioned in him. 'I'm confident.'

'I wish I bloody well was,' Ferguson yelled, as all hell seemed to descend on the beach ahead, as, added to the inferno of the bombs and shells, came the whoosh and obscene howl of myriad rockets being fired from what their Canadian gunners called 'mattresses', packed rows of tubes which could fire hundreds of rockets in a handful of seconds. Now the whole beach was being rapidly swallowed up by thick black smoke, slashed here and there by sudden spurts of bright cheery red flame. 'I can't see a bloody thing...' He flashed a glance at the green-glowing dial of his wristwatch. In thirty minutes precisely the first wave of the South Lancs and the East Yorks of the Iron Division would hit the beaches. Time was running out fast. They had to get to that channel and start working their way to that damned bunker.

Carl the comedian felt comfortable and relatively safe for the first time since his E-boat had entered the English Channel. He doubted if the Tommies' radar could detect him easily at the speed he was going, and if it did there was little the enemy could do about it. For now the whole coastline was shrouded by thick black smoke and the smoke was spreading out to the sea. As he saw it, the smoke was just as effective as a proper man-made smoke screen.

The German *Kriegsmarine* couldn't have

done a better job. He bent and called down the voice tube to the engineer below, 'Half speed – both, *Obermaat*.'

'Half speed it is, *Herr Leutnant*,' came the reply. The E-boat slowed down immediately, her sharp prow dropping to the water.

Carl knew he was taking a chance. Still, it was a chance worth taking. Ahead of him the dark horizon was packed with enemy ships; they stretched from port to starboard as far as the eye could see. He had never had a target like this. He couldn't miss once he had picked out a suitable 'kill' and launched his 'tin fish', his deadly magnetic torpedoes. 'Lucky me,' he chortled to no one in particular. 'This day I'm going to *cure my throat-ache**.' He pressed the E-boat's siren. The instrument shrilled its warning to the crew. They knew what it meant. Crazy Carl and his three tits were going into the attack.

*Slang expression for the 'Knight's Cross', worn around the neck.

237

Two

Now the assault infantry of the Iron Division were almost there. Some of them were still vomiting into their brown paper bags. Some smoked nervously. Others tried to talk, make the usual cracks. But it was almost impossible in the tremendous noise. Overhead, great fifteen inch shells from the warships ripped the dawn apart with the sound of giant pieces of canvas being torn. To their front the pall of brown smoke was stabbed here and there by scarlet flames and the flashes of the enemy cannon answering. Machine-gun bullets zipped the length of the beach. Everywhere the grey-green water was already littered with debris, abandoned equipment, shattered Rommel's asparagus, men floating on their faces, nudged back and forth by the swell.

The first blunt-nosed landing craft hit the beach. Soldiers sprang out. Sometimes they were chest-high in the cold water, rifles held at the port, spreading to left and right as they had been trained to do. After all, they had been practising – some of them – for four years for this moment. And a good few of them lived only for that single moment, before they hit the wet sand, dead already. For now the hidden German machine guns were sweeping the beach from side to side, stuttering frantically, pouring slugs at the attackers at a tremendous rate.

But a lot of them made it to the first obstacle: lines of rusting barbed wire, mine-fields and the Rommel's asparagus with their deadly charges attached, now high above the water. As they fell to the sand, the living among the dead, they cast anxious looks to their rear. They were waiting for the first amphibious tanks to come waddling ashore, shedding their waterproof canvas screens as they did so, ready to attack the first bunkers with their 75mm cannon. There they were, shedding their water wings. Behind them came tight, grim bunches of infantry, ignoring the hail of pebbles and sand flung up by the tanks' churning tracks, grateful for the protection of that life-saving armour.

Still the German machine guns sang their song of death. Everywhere the men of the South Lancs and East Yorks fell, the unfashionable regiments which had been chosen to be the first to step into their bath of blood. In front of the tanks the beach was now being transformed into a khaki carpet of dead and dying northern infantry. Still the tanks were coming on, crawling forward at their deliberate pace, cannon twitching from side to side like the snouts of predatory monsters seeking out their prey.

The first Sherman was hit. There was the hollow boom of steel striking steel. The tank came to an abrupt stop, its right trail reeling out behind it like a severed limb. Next to the crippled tank, black smoke pouring from its ruptured engine with tiny greedy tongues of flame already licking up from the cowling, another driver panicked. He swung the thirty-ton tank round out of the line of fire, lost control and went ploughing through a line of advancing infantry. They didn't have a chance. The tank thrashed its way through them, grinding them to a bloody pulp under its tracks. Crazy with grief and anger, the platoon leader rushed at the now stalled tank and started beating it with his cane, crying, 'They're my men. For God's sake, see what you've done to my poor soldiers!' Next moment a shell slammed into the stalled Sherman. Both it and the grief-stricken platoon leader vanished in an angry burst of violent scarlet flame.

Now the infantry were struggling through the first lines of barbed wire. Some remembered their training. They pelted full length at it, arms outstretched, and let themselves be impaled upon it like some khaki-clad Christ. Others followed. They ran up the figures of the men fixed to the wire, vaulted to the other side and continued running, firing as they went. Others forgot everything they had learned in training these last years and tried to worm their way under the wire, while the machine guns chattered mercilessly, picking them off by the dozen, the score, and in the end by the hundred. Casualties were mounting rapidly, and despite the attackers' enormous superiority they were still not through the first major obstacle and then on to the line of bunkers just waiting for them...

'We who are about to die, salute thee, o flag!' Crazy Carl yelled above the noise, and gave his absurd banner a silly salute. Then he pulled his battered white cap more firmly down on his cropped blond head and cried down the voice tube, '*Los*, you asparagus Tarzans down there. Let me have some juice

... and don't frigging well let me down or I'll have the nuts off'n yer with a blunt razor blade.' The terrible threat worked. The deck trembled once more under his feet. The E-boat's prow rose sharply. In an instant she was cleaving her way through the waves at a tremendous pace, heading for the great fleet of enemy ships ahead.

Tracer, hard, cold and bright white, started to zip towards the attacking E-boats in a lethal morse. Somewhere a 40mm quick-firer began to pound away. Star shells exploded above the slow-moving convoy, and for the first time, it seemed, the Tommy ships became aware that they were actually being attacked.

Shells exploded on either side of Crazy Carl's craft, which was zigzagging wildly, its radio seemingly touching the water as the skipper flung the wheel from side to side in his attempt to dodge the incoming fire.

'Perverted banana suckers!' Carl cried wildly, carried away by the whole lunatic business of combat. 'You need to get up earlier to get old Carl, arses with ears!' In that same instant a great gout of water swamped the front of the craft and gave him a cold shower, leaving him gasping and spluttering, yet full of determination to sink as many of these damned impertinent Tommies as he could before his turn came.

An ammunition ship was hit to port. It went up in a crazy rush of explosives, red, white, green. A great flame seared the length of the dying ship like that of a giant blowtorch. Maverick shells went zigzagging in a dozen different directions. A moment later there was a mighty crunch and the ship disintegrated totally.

Crazy Carl cheered and started to select his own target. But before he got that far, there was a great hush like an express rushing at top speed through a deserted station at midnight. The E-boat rocked wildly. Here and there great red hot shards of steel tumbled to her deck. A seaman was hit. He screamed once. Next moment his severed head, complete with helmet, rolled into the scuppers like a football abandoned by a careless child.

'Holy mackerel,' Crazy Carl yelled. 'The rotten swine. Hard to port!' He swung the wheel round himself. The radio mast touched the water as the second great shell missed the E-boat by metres. Shaking the water out of his eyes, Carl caught a glimpse of a lean grey shape heading straight for him, smoke streaming from her stacks, her forward cannon belching fire.

Instinctively he knew the Tommy destroyer would ram him in the last instant if she didn't hit his E-boat before that. Comedian that he was, Crazy Carl knew that he wasn't going to fool with an enemy craft three times his size and with four times his firepower. At this range he wouldn't even bring his torpedoes to bear. Flight was called for while his ship was still in one piece.

It was thus that Crazy Carl unwittingly started to steer a wild course for his confrontation with a battered old tub at the edge of the invasion fleet, on which he wouldn't normally have wasted a single burst of machine gun fire...

As one, Ferguson and Seagram flung up their binoculars. Around them all was chaos and confusion. Star shells exploded above the sea in silver brilliance. Tracer hissed back and forth in multicoloured splendour. The roar of the high-speed attacking E-boats, dragging huge white wakes behind them, mingled with the yammer of the defenders' guns firing at a tremendous rate. All hell had been let loose and Ferguson realized immediately that they had walked into some kind of a trap that threatened the success of their whole operation, perhaps even that of the beach assault.

'Charlie,' he moaned above the awesome racket, 'can't you get any more speed out of this old tub of yours?'

Another shell hissed above the old tug. Her for'ard mast went. It came tumbling down in a shower of blue electric sparks. A rating trying to make a break for it screamed shrilly as the heavy wooden and steel beam smashed into his body, knocking him to the debris-littered deck; his blood splattered about him immediately in a crimson star.

'I'm trying, Peter,' Seagram yelled back. 'I'm trying to get every last bit of power out of her. I shouldn't be surprised if her bloody boiler doesn't go bust at any moment.'

'All right, all right, Charlie.' Ferguson calmed himself, repressed his anger and tried to soothe the younger man. He knew the signs of old. He didn't want Seagram cracking up, now that he believed he had got him off the booze once more. 'Just let's play it cool. We'll make it.' Then he couldn't quite contain himself, and burst out with, *'We've bloody well got to, Charlie.'*

Now they were leaving the bulk of the transports carrying the doomed remaining companies of the East Yorks and the South

245

Lancs. At a steady eight knots they headed for the shallows, ploughing their way through the smoke and the violent sudden flashes of exploding artillery shells, trying to find that vital inlet that would lead them to the hidden bunker, waiting to slaughter the surviving assault infantry once they had succeeded in breaking through the first line of beach defences...

To their right on the beach, the survivors of these unfashionable provincial infantry regiments were beginning to clear the beach. Behind them they left their dead. The carnage had been appalling. Everywhere the beaches were strewn with their dead, killed before they could fire a shot at the unseen enemy. Now they lay in their sack-like stiffened postures. Some lay sprawled in extravagant poses in the wet sand, fists clenched, faces contorted as if in great anger; others seemed little more than bloodstained bundles of battered wet khaki caught up in the rusting German wire; a few simply lay there, apparently unharmed, not a mark on them, as if they were taking a gentle nap.

But there was no time to mourn the dead, which included both regimental colonels, who had trained the dead for years and were now dead themselves, within minutes of landing in France. The survivors were beginning their assault on the seawall, which lay in front of the bunkers with their waiting machine-gun crews. They had done this sort of thing before many a time. But that had been during an exercise; this was the real thing. Bren guns were placed at regular intervals along the dripping stone wall. They would, in theory, cover the assault as the first wave crossed the seawall and rushed the barbed wire beyond. In theory.

Now the first volunteers approached the wall, their weapons gripped in hands that were damp with sweat. 'All right, lads,' their NCOs called above the snap-and-crack of small arms fire, 'gonna be as easy as falling off a log! GO!'

They went and began falling at once, crying for their mothers, cursing, screaming in their dying agony, falling off the 'logs' from which there was no rising. Still, the old habit of discipline, obedience, the honour of the regiment, comradeship kept them going. Others took their places and were hit, too, as that cruel machine-gun fire swept the top of the wall. They started to pile up like heaps of wood. Still they kept going, so that now the rear ranks were crawling up the dead bodies of their comrades, as if up some ghastly stairs. Behind them a handful of mortarmen set up their three-inch mortar and commenced lobbing bombs over the heads of their hard-pressed comrades on the seawall, trying to knock out the machine gunners.

The fact that these mortarmen were returning the enemy's murderous fire encouraged the survivors. Under the cover of their Bren guns, more and more of them managed to cross the wall and continue the advance towards the bunkers. But still they were taking serious casualties and those still in command, now mostly junior captains and even second lieutenants, replacing the colonels and majors already mown down with the first wave, knew that soon they'd meet that 'hidden bunker', as they all called it. Then the real hell would start...

Three

'Stand by engine room!' Crazy Carl yelled down the voice tube. He picked up his loudhailer and addressed the deck, 'Torpedo mates stand by. Quick-firer stand by!' His veterans, most of them in reality callow

248

youths who had yet to begin to shave properly, rammed their helmets down harder and waited for the skipper's orders.

All around them there was total chaos. Through the dark brown smoke they caught glimpses of E-boats skimming and turning wildly as they shot up and down the convoy selecting their targets. Already they had knocked out another fat Tommy transport. It listed heavily to one side and men were springing wildly from its upper deck. Below, tanks, trying to escape the flames leaping up from its aft, were plunging into the water at the ramp and were sinking like stones. A Tommy destroyer was now attempting to cover the grievously hurt ship and its men. Slicing through the water in circles, it was trying to lay a heavy smokescreen and at the same time dodge the torpedoes hissing towards it.

Crazy Carl would have dearly loved to have tackled the Tommy destroyer himself. But he knew he daren't do that; the destroyer was the selected target of his flotilla leader. 'I don't think he'd like it if I put a tin fish up her arse first,' he said to no one particular, and then resigned himself to dealing with the rusty old tug before he went and found another more suitable victim.

So he went through his usual ritual. *'Le style c' est l' homme,'* he told himself in bad French, as he tilted his battered cap to a more rakish angle and pulled the white silk muffler tighter round his neck, knowing that with a bit of luck he'd never wear the scarf again; for a scarf would hide the Knight's Cross or the Iron Cross that would be hanging from his throat. Finally he dashed some cheap cologne around his face. It would kill the stink of oil and vomit. As an afterthought he grabbed the bottle of cheap Korn he always kept on the bridge and took a hefty swig of the stuff. He felt the cheap gin slam against his gullet and then burn its way down to his ruined stomach. The pain there vanished immediately. 'That'll keep the spew down for a while,' he said, again to no one in particular, and then concentrated on his 'kill' soon to come.

His plan of attack was simple – and highly dangerous. The E-boat would race in at top speed: forty knots. He would use the craft itself as a direction finder for his torpedoes – his 'kippers', as the crew called them. He wouldn't order his torpedo mate to fire them till they were five hundred metres away from the tug. It was a dangerous tactic, he knew. At forty knots he would be unlikely to spot any obstacles in his path. Too, steering a dead straight course, he'd be a fairly easy target for any enemy gunner once the Tommy had lined him up in his sights. But it was a risk he was prepared to take for that black and white piece of tin he'd love to have dangling from his throat this June.

Then he forgot the 'tin'. The adrenalin started to work. His whole body seemed to tingle electrically. It was as if he had just drunk a whole bottle of champers, fast. He grinned at his reflection in the glass protective screen in front of him on the bridge and yelled down the voice tube. *'Motorraum ... Voller Dampf voraus!'*

The E-boat lurched forward at once. He grabbed a stanchion to support himself. The roar of the motors was ear splitting. The very air quivered with their vibration. A huge white wave curved up on both sides of the lean, deadly craft like great swan's wings. Speedily the deck tilted upwards as the sharp bow rose from the water. On the deck, now awash with spray and water, the torpedo men steadied themselves the best they could against the vibrations, gaze intent on the skipper on the bridge under his absurd flag. They knew their job. At the signal they would have to fire immediately, for the crazy young *Leutnant* would break to left or right to avoid enemy fire.

Now the old tug with its sandbagged bridge and bow seemed to fill the whole horizon. It didn't, but it was all that Crazy Carl could see. He even fancied he could make out the faces of the men on her bridge. Routinely and automatically he ducked now. The Tommies manning the light machine guns on her deck were firing all out. White and green tracer was zipping across the surface of the sea, dragging its burning light after it. Crazy Carl prayed the bullets wouldn't hit his torpedo crews; then all the effort and death-defying bravery on their part would be for nothing.

Slugs ripped the length of the superstructure. Glass and metal burst under that terrific hail of steel. A rating flung up his hands in mortal agony and went over the side without a sound. Another fell to the littered deck, howling like a trapped animal, his hands full of red gore as he tried to hold in his guts, which were slithering from his shattered stomach like a grey steaming serpent. 'Open up quick-firer!' Crazy Carl yelled above the tremendous noise. 'Give the buck-toothed British bastards some of their own medicine!'

The crew of the deadly Vierling flak, a four-barrelled anti-aircraft gun, needed no urging. The slugs were whining off the gun's metal shield in all directions. It was a marvel that none of them had been hit yet. The gun-layer went to work with a will. The gun blasted into action, as Crazy Carl started to count off the distance between his E-boat and the tug. *Seven hundred ... six hundred ... five hundred and fifty metres ...* It would not be long now. Crazy Carl tensed. A couple of seconds more and he'd fire the 'kippers' and that would be that...

Ferguson grabbed the wounded engineer and dragged him back in a slither of blood behind the sandbags. Forty millimetre tracer shells were coming his way in a solid wall of sudden death. The Hun had turned one of their murderous Vierling flak cannon on the tug. Shrapnel hissed everywhere, glowing an evil red.

Now bent double, he ran back to the gun. He slammed it into his right shoulder, feeling a sense of power as he did so. He was in a position to fight. It was up to young Charlie to bring the ship into the inlet before the damned E-boat racing toward them at a tremendous speed could scupper the old tub.

He peered down the ring sight. He had the E-boat dead centre. The Hun was making no attempt to dodge the fire coming from the tug. Perhaps the unknown German skipper was contemptuous of the defenders' fire. He controlled his breathing as he had been taught to do and said to himself, 'All right, you Nazi bastard, try this on for size.' Next moment he pressed the trigger. The butt of the Bren gun kicked back into his shoulder. His nostrils were abruptly assailed by the stink of burned cordite.

The burst from the Bren gun ripped the length of the speeding boat. Wood splintered. A radio mast came down in a fury of blue electrical sparks. Below, German ratings screamed as the debris fell on them. Ferguson didn't care. He was carried away by the mad, unreasoning blood lust of battle. He ripped off the empty magazine and slapped another one home in the Bren. This time he controlled his emotions more effectively. He was determined to put the E-boat out of action before it closed completely with the battered old tug. Once the E-boat did so, he knew they didn't stand a chance of completing their mission. They'd blow Seagram's rusty old tub clear out of the water.

'*Three hundred and fifty metres!*' Crazy Carl yelled above the thud-thud of the quick-firing. All around him there was noise and chaos. Virtually all the deck ratings had been hit. The deck was a bloody mess of dead and dying sailors. Still the rest carried on. Out of the corner of his eye he saw that the torpedomen were still in position, a couple of them bleeding from their wounds, but ready to fire their tin fish all the same. He raised his arm. The critical moment had come. '*Obermaat,*' he began, in the same instant that Ferguson fired again.

The tracer raced towards the E-boat like a blazing white wall. It enveloped the young skipper. He staggered, barely aware of the burning pain everywhere; the shock was too great. 'Oh, my arse—' He began. Then he could speak no more. His mouth was abruptly full of the copper taste of his blood. He choked and coughed. A stream of red shot to the littered, torn deck. He went down on his knees, gasping and choking like a boxer refusing to go down for the count. '*Skipper,*' someone cried.

Dimly, Crazy Carl was aware that someone was trying to help. He could see the ashen-faced rating through a wavering red mist.

With blood-red claws, still on his knees, Carl pushed him away weakly. 'Leave ... leave me ... alone.' The dying skipper could hear his voice coming from far, far away. He knew he was finished. He'd never 'cure his throatache' now. 'Ram ... helmsman ... ram the ... Tommy bastard...'

'Sir,' the man at the wheel began to protest.

The skipper didn't give him a chance. Dying as he was, he knew that at the range they were now the tin fish would be useless. The E-boat would have to stop the tug by ramming, even if it sank the wooden craft. There was no other way...

Ferguson had been hit – badly. He knew that instinctively. He had been hit before. But never this bad. He had lost all strength in his left arm. It was hanging from his side uselessly, the thick hot blood pouring down its length. He tried to keep hold of the Bren gun. To no avail. He just didn't have the strength any more. 'God Almighty,' he groaned as the E-boat loomed up again out of a sudden cloud of smoke. She was still heading straight for the tug, her deck shattered as was most of her superstructure. As weak and close to oblivion as Ferguson was, though, it was clear to him that the E-boat wouldn't give up now. She'd sink the tug if it was the last thing she accomplished on this earth. Ferguson knew that all right.

'Peter, old friend.' It was Charlie Seagram, voice full of emotion as he gazed down at the man who had given him new hope and then befriended him. 'Is it ... bad?'

Ferguson bit his bottom lip till the blood came. The pain was bloody awful, but he mustn't let Charlie know that. The young naval officer had to carry out the rest of the mission without him. He needed no other worries. 'No,' he lied. 'Just catching my second wind.'

'But you're bleeding all over, Peter.'

'Always looks worse than it is when you're wounded.' He winced as the pain stabbed his guts again like a thrust of a red-hot poker. 'The quacks'll soon patch me up again...' He raised his voice and attempted to smile, but failed miserably.

'Just you carry on with the job, Charlie ... I'm afraid I'm not much use to you any more ... Get on with it.'

Charlie Seagram looked down at the sapper colonel. Ferguson sounded as if he were confident that he'd survive, but he wondered. He'd seen dying men before at Dunkirk in what now seemed another age. Ferguson looked to him as if he were going to suffer the same fate. His eyes were rolling upwards and there was that thin white pinched look of the nose that he had associated with impending death since Dunkirk back in '40.

'But I can't leave you—' he commenced.

Ferguson cut him short with an almost savage snorted, 'Don't fuck around, Seagram. Get to it – and that's an order.'

Seagram hesitated no longer. There was nothing he could do for Ferguson at this moment. The sooner he carried out their mission and got the sapper colonel to an MO the better. 'Hold on, Peter ... hold on, Peter!' he yelled, and then he was stepping over the debris, trying to ignore the dead sappers and sailors that littered the deck now back to the shattered bridge. He'd do it, he told himself; he'd save Ferguson...

A few hundred metres away, Crazy Carl was dying too and trying to hang on till the end of the attack. 'I've got to,' he commanded himself, as the black veil of death started to descend upon him, *'I've just got to!'* The conviction was so tremendous – he didn't know why – that hot tears welled in his eyes, and momentarily blinded him.

But Crazy Carl was not fated to hang on to

the end of the battle. One of the tug's gunners struck lucky. In the very instant that the tug reeled under a direct hit, the unknown British gunner's shell slammed into the E boat like a blow from a gigantic fist. The impact was so tremendous that Carl yelled out loud with agony. His bones splintered. Blood splattered the deck in bright red gobs. Urine and faeces streamed down his broken legs. For one fleeting moment, as he lay there, all spirit fleeing his ruined body, his young, hard face softened into a kind of weary smile. Next moment the E-boat careened into the tug with the force of some massive factory steam hammer.

For what seemed an age, the two craft just wallowed there in the boiling water. The E-boat had been transformed into a mass of grotesquely twisted metal, her bow crumpled stupidly like a squashed banana. Everywhere there lay dead men scattered on all sides like broken toys cast away by a careless spoiled child. *'My black tits,'* he whispered for some reason, and wished his tin fish had exploded on impact. But now he knew it was too late; they wouldn't. It had all been in vain. He sighed.

Almost in the same instant that the remaining petty officers started to shrill their whistles, to tell the survivors to abandon ship, there was a monstrous groaning like some huge beast in pain. With a tearing and a shearing of metal, the E-boat broke away from the embrace of the stalled tug. Her end was not dramatic. She didn't sink immediately. Instead she disintegrated, as if in slow motion, her stern rearing high into the air, her screws spinning uselessly, while her bow dipped itself below the surface of the debris littered sea.

'Abandon ship!' someone called in a broken voice. But there were no survivors left to do so.

Then, with startling suddenness, the E-boat's main magazine exploded. The broken-backed craft was racked by the shudder of exploding shells and other ammunition from stem to stern. Great gleaming silver fissures opened up everywhere. Tracer ammunition zigzagged crazily in bursts of bright silver, red and green straight into the air like a lethal fireworks display, and then it was all over and the 'three black tits' disappeared beneath the waves.

Four

'Colonel Ferguson's dead, sir,' the tough-looking sapper sergeant with his arm in a bloodstained sling reported.

Seagram didn't seem able to take in the information properly, for his young face showed no emotion, as if the death of his friend meant nothing to him. 'Other officers?' he asked.

'All dead or badly wounded, sir ... None of them in a fit state to do the job.'

Seagram knew what the 'job' was. He frowned. In the corner of the shattered bridge a rating, shot through the hand, was lapping up GS rum out of a tin bowl greedily, like a thirsty dog. Seagram envied him. He wished he could do the same. The sapper sergeant followed the direction of the gaze and commented sardonically, 'That stuff's not going to do him much good.'

'Why not?' Seagram rounded on him. 'Wish I could get a gut full of it. That's the only way out of this bloody mess.'

The sapper took it in his stride. 'It is for him, definitely.'

'What's that bloody well supposed to mean, Sergeant?' Seagram demanded.

' 'Cos he's bought one in the guts, sir. Saw it myself. Bullet in yer guts and booze.' He shook his head. 'Tough titty – yer a goner.'

'Perhaps it's better that way.' Seagram looked longingly at the bowl of rum. How easy it would be, he told himself. Get stewed and let somebody else take the responsibility, even if the rum killed you. After all, those who would have to carry on were going to get killed anyhow. Why not take the easier way of snuffing it?

'Sir, it's up to you.' The sergeant interrupted his reverie. 'And we ain't got much time left. Old Jerry's ranging in on us already. Mortar bombs.' He indicated the sudden spurt of sand and water close to their port bow as the first of the mortar bombs came howling out of the sky and exploded nearby. 'Another one to starboard and the Jerries'll have us nice and tidy ranged in.'

Seagram dismissed the sailor drinking out of the bowl, the blood pouring out of his mouth and mixing with the rum. 'Right then, Sarge. Get your lads together straight away. We'll have a bash.'

'Good show, sir,' the Sarge yelled back above the obscene howl of another batch of mortar bombs falling out of the sky like lethal black eggs. 'We'll get the bastards, never you fear, sir.'

Five minutes later soldiers and a handful of sailors who had volunteered to go were dropping over the side of the stalled tug, while on the deck the dying drunken sailor was still trying to lap up the rum and singing at the same time, 'Tight as a drum ... never been done ... Queen of all the fairies ... Isn't it a pity she's only one titty to feed the baby on ... Poor little bugger's only...'

Seagram as a naval officer was naturally not used to land fighting. Still, he knew enough to ensure that his mixed force was protected from the enemy fire ranging in on them for as long as possible. Thus he ordered the sapper sergeant to keep the men moving forward under the leeside of the tug, which was taking the brunt of the shelling from the hidden bunker. Soon, of course, they'd have to leave the shelter of the tug and wade their way up the rest of the inlet. Then they'd be out in the open, with a minefield to cross before they could launch their attack. As he remembered poor dead Peter Ferguson saying at one of the pre-D-Day briefings, 'Then we'll have to move like greased lightning. In like Flynn. No stopping for casualties. No stopping for anything. If only a handful of us reach the bunker, then we've done it. A couple of satchel charges through the bloody place's gun-ports and old Jerry'll be pleading to surrender.'

Seagram sniffed as he moved through the water at the head of the file of soldiers and sailors. It had all sounded very easy the way Peter had put it. But then he had been a trained sapper and soldier. Seagram was a mere sailor who had last fired a handgun in training back in '39. Still, the job had to be done; and, if he survived, he had Sally Ann and her love to look forward to.

Thus they advanced, each man wrapped in a cocoon of his own thoughts, hopes, and apprehensions, believing as young men do that the worst will never happen to them, but to the next man. Above them the old tug rocked to and fro violently, as the bunker's big guns started to pound her to pieces. Here and there Seagram could still hear the slow chatter of the British Bren gun which contrasted with the hysterical high-pitched *brr-brr* of the German Spandaus ripping the length of the ship's bow. He guessed that the

British gunners wouldn't last much longer under such intense fire. What would happen then? Would the Germans in the bunker turn their attention on the South Lancs, who would be coming up behind them? If they did, Seagram wouldn't give the South Lancs infantry much of a chance of surviving. And then what? The success of the whole Iron Division landing would be at stake. The thought lent urgency to Seagram's advance. He turned to the sergeant behind him and yelled, hands clapped around his mouth, 'Keep 'em moving fast, Sarge ... We'll be clearing the tug's bow at any moment.'

'Righty-ho, sir,' the sergeant returned cheerfully, almost as if he were enjoying this deadly advance and what was soon to come. 'Bash on regardless, eh?'

'Yes, bash on regardless,' Seagram echoed the old army phrase, but with far less enthusiasm in his voice than the big sapper sergeant.

He reached the rusty battered edge of the bow. He paused. Above him the slow fire of the last Bren had ceased. The gunner was either dead or had run out of ammunition. They were on their own. Now the Jerries would abandon the tug to its fate; it no longer played any role in the invasion. Seagram licked lips which had become very dry. Behind him his little force started to bunch up. 'Problems, sir?' the NCO asked. Seagram didn't answer. He couldn't. Now, however, he steeled himself to look round the edge of the bow.

There it was, almost parallel with the earth on the left side of the inlet: a squat grey shape, twin metal cupolas on its roof, spitting scarlet fire with other firing holes on each side of the thick concrete. Around it there were at least three barriers of rusty barbed wire, and beyond that a single wire with little metal plates attached to it at regular intervals. Seagram couldn't see what was written on the plates, but he could make out the design on them well enough. It was a black skull and crossbones, and sailor that he was he knew what that design signified. It was a minefield: the one that Ferguson had mentioned. He bit his bottom lip uncertainly. Behind him the sapper said reassuringly, 'Don't worry, we can tackle that baby with our eyes shut. Besides, sir, perhaps old Jerry has forgotten to extend the mines into and across the inlet. It's gonna be roses, roses all the way.'

Famous last words, Seagram said to himself.

Aloud he said, with more confidence than he felt, 'I'm sure you're right, Sarge. Come on.' He took a deep breath and moved out of the cover provided by the battered stranded tug, half expecting to be shot immediately.

Nothing happened. Through the drifting fog of war covering the beach and the strand beyond, he could see the typical coal-scuttle helmets of German soldiers, crouching and firing their weapons and then moving ever backwards towards the little town which was the Iron Division's first objective on this sector of the beach. But none of them seemed the slightest bit interested in the single file of British soldiers and sailors wading along the inlet, heading for the bunker.

Behind Seagram, the sapper sergeant whispered, 'Piece o' cake, sir. The Jerries haven't spotted—' He never finished the sentence. To their right a couple of helmeted heads appeared above the bank, yelled something in German and then the firing broke out almost immediately.

Behind the sergeant, the sapper corporal with that terrible round pack of instant death on his shoulders reacted immediately. Without orders, he brought up the muzzle of the short length of piping attached to the round pack and pressed the trigger. *Whoosh!*

267

There was a sound like some primeval monster breathing hard. A vicious stab of scarlet flame. The air was abruptly filled with the acrid stink of burning. Up the bank the grass shrivelled and went black immediately. The two heads did the same. Faces contorted in the rictus of death, the Germans shrieked as their flesh bubbled and blackened, the skin splitting in that tremendous heat into scarlet streaks. They were dead before they slithered over the embankment into the water.

Seagram retched drily, his shoulders heaving. He wanted to vomit, but he couldn't. Next to him the NCO said, 'Good work, Chalky. That warmed the buggers up sharpish.'

Smiling modestly, the scarlet-faced corporal carrying the flame-thrower said, 'We aim to please, Sarge.'

Seagram had had enough. 'Stop blethering,' he snapped. 'You're like two bloody old biddies. Move it!'

Gingerly, very gingerly, Seagram approached the line of wire which he knew now bordered the German minefield protecting the sunken bunker. Behind him the sapper sergeant and the corporal bearing that terrible flame-thrower on his back were no longer so sanguine. They were sappers;

they knew just how dangerous and unpredictable minefields were. Besides, they had managed to rescue only one mine detector from the damaged sinking tug. If they had to clear a path through the mines to reach the bunker, they'd have to do it with their bare hands and bayonets. That would be a wearisome and dreadfully dangerous task.

Now, hardly daring to breathe, Seagram in the lead came right up to the wire. The sign in German was quite clear now: ACHTUNG MINEN!; and for those who couldn't read German, that black skull and crossbones clearly indicated the fate of those who wandered unprepared beyond that single rusty wire. Seagram placed one foot carefully in front of the other, hardly daring to disturb the dirty brown water, knowing that if they had miscalculated he could step on one of the devilish devices concealed by the water the very next moment.

He took another step forward. Behind him the others tensed, crouching a little, as if they expected an explosion at any moment. Seagram started to sweat, despite the dawn cold. He could feel the cold beads of sweat trickling down the small of his back unpleasantly. His hands were beginning to tremble with the tension, too. He prayed for safety as he had never prayed before.

Suddenly, startlingly, he felt his foot grate against something – something metallic. 'Oh my God,' he gasped out loud.

The sapper sergeant reacted at once. 'Don't move, sir!' he commanded with an air of authority. 'Not an inch ... keep your foot exactly where it is.'

'Is it a mine?' Seagram said through gritted teeth, his leg frozen.

'Sounded like it,' the sergeant replied, as he unsheathed his bayonet. 'Here we go – and, sir, please don't move, or we're both for the chop.' He bent, and taking a deep breath ducked his head beneath the dirty brown water. He took hold of Seagram's slightly raised right leg and, feeling his way down it like a lover might do some shapely female limb, felt for Seagram's boot and what lay beneath it. Next moment he rose, spluttering a little, to announce, 'A bloody bouncing Betty.'

Seagram started to breathe hard and fast. His heart raced. The right side of his face began to twitch. The thought that in a moment the mine could blow his leg off and make him a cripple for the rest of his life was impossible – unbearable. But with an effort of sheer naked willpower he pulled himself

270

together. In a shaky voice that he hardly recognized as his own, he asked, 'What's the drill now, Sarge?'

'First we keep calm, sir. If you don't move an inch, I'll tackle it. I've defused the buggers before. They're tricky – three prongs to get round. But it can be done.'

'Fast?'

'Yes fast, sir ... as long as you don't move.'

'I won't, I promise you. Get cracking please.'

The sergeant hesitated no longer. 'Here we go, sir,' he announced. Next moment he ducked beneath the surface of the muddy brown water. Above it, Seagram bit his bottom lip till the blood came, wishing fervently that he could down a swift shot of strong whisky to calm his tingling nerves, but knowing that was impossible. He'd just have to stick it out without alcohol...

The colonel of the South Lancs knew he couldn't wait much longer. His men were being slaughtered where they lay in the sand, awaiting the order to advance. His lead company was almost wiped out already and they had still not secured their first objectives. He cursed under his breath, but his face revealed nothing of his emotions to his troops surrounding him on the beach. He knew a good leader should never show tension or inner doubt.

Again he looked at the green glowing dial of his watch. He'd give those naval chaps another five minutes at the most, then, if the bunker had not been secured by then, he'd attack. God knows what the casualties would be. But there was no other choice. The rest of the brigade would already be disembarking on the beaches behind him. After them would come the medics, the Service Corps, engineers and all the rest of the support troops. In his imagination he visualized thousands of men and vehicles piling up right across the Channel and deep into south-eastern England, waiting for him and his South Lancs. Perhaps even Monty himself was' tensed in his caravan head-quarters near Portsmouth, willing the South Lancs to get on and take their objectives so that his old Iron Division could move inland. God, what a mess!

To his right one of his men was crying, sobbing and sobbing, as if his very heart would break. The colonel, who had another half hour to live, could not bring himself to turn and look.

Five

'Gently does it, sir,' the sergeant warned, gasping for breath as he came up from under the water. In his hand he held the bouncing Betty, the landmine of which the troops joked, 'Get hit by that in the crotch, mate, and yer can forget about the other – yer dick'll have disappeared.' Carefully he lobbed the defused mine into the embankment. 'Shall I go first, sir?'

Seagram stopped himself shaking. As firmly as he could he said, 'Thanks, Sarge. You did a good job. No, I'll go first.' He added with a grim attempt at gallows humour, 'They say rank hath its privileges. I'm claiming my right to have my head blown off first as the ranking officer.'

The NCO smiled wearily. 'Right you are, sir. But we'd better have the bloke with the Piat up just behind us – in case.'

'OK.' Seagram was not familiar with the strange infantry weapon, a tube which fired a Piat-shaped explosive bomb meant to knock out tanks, but he knew why the sapper NCO had made the suggestion. Soon they'd be closing with the sunken bunker and the Piat would be the only weapon they possessed capable of tackling the bunker's firing slits set in thick ferro-concrete.

So they pushed towards their final date with destiny, wading through up the muddy inlet, concealed to both sides by the high verges, but still aware of the battle raging all around them. Now they were bent like farm labourers returning home after a hard day in the fields, each man laden and bowed with equipment. Naturally they knew they'd be discovered sooner or later. Still, they took unnecessary and elaborate steps to conceal their progress, despite the constant thunder of war from the sea and the answering fire of the German defenders.

Step by step they advanced ever closer to the still unseen bunker. At Seagram's heels, the sergeant kept prodding the bottom with his bayonet, ever alert to that scraping of metal against metal which would indicate another mine beneath them; while the lad carrying the Piat now held the ugly weapon across his chest, as if he couldn't fire it soon enough. And all, sailor and soldier, were tense, awaiting that first challenge, the angry shout, the crack of a rifle bullet which would indicate they had been discovered, which inevitably they would be sooner or later.

But when that moment came, it did so totally unexpectedly and from a quarter that they had not anticipated. Suddenly, as they turned a bend in the inlet, wading waist-deep in the dark brown water, a wildly swaying figure came towards them, one hand outstretched like a blind man, crying in English, 'Don't go on, mates. It's no ruddy use. Don't go on, mates – *Oh for God's sake, don't go on!*'

Seagram stumbled to a stop, caught completely by surprise. Next to him the sapper sergeant did the same, hissing, 'He's gone barmy, sir. The poor bugger.' He put up his free hand and pushed against the stranger's chest. 'Now son, what's this here?'

The stranger seemed totally unaware of their presence. It was as if he didn't even feel the sergeant's restraining hand. Again he repeated that strange litany, 'It's no ruddy use ... For God's sake, don't go on...'

Abruptly the sergeant lost patience with the soldier, who was obviously suffering from battle fatigue. 'Now stop this little lark of yours,' he hissed threateningly, 'or I'll have you on a fizzer. You'll bloody well give us away in half a mo, rabbiting on like you are. Stop it!'

The half-crazy lost soldier reacted totally differently from how the NCO expected. The quavering, self-pitying note vanished from his voice abruptly, as he cried, 'Don't you bloody well talk to me like that. You don't know what I've been through.' Suddenly he pushed the sergeant's chest. Caught off guard, the sapper staggered backwards. Next moment the lost soldier was clambering up the muddy embankment, crying at the top of his voice, 'You've had it ... all of you've had it. They're going—' He never finished his prediction. Outlined by the stark dawn light on the top of the embankment, the bullets ripped his chest into a series of blood-red button holes. He staggered wildly, as if he might fall back into the water. He caught himself just in time, and staggered on, dying on his feet, mumbling, 'You've had it ... you've had it...'

Now the damage had been done. Almost instantly whistles started to shrill the alarm. A deep bass voice cried urgently. *'Los ... Los, Manner ... Die Tommies sind daunten!'* The cry was followed by a stick grenade whistling down from above to explode in a burst of vicious red at the end of the little column.

Seagram attacked at once. There was no need for further concealment. Followed by the sergeant and the kid armed with the Piat, he flung himself over the edge of the embankment while the rest of his group commenced firing. Only yards ahead lay the bunker in all its grey ugly menace.

'Blast the ports!' he cried urgently, as fire exploded in scarlet fury from the bunker's roof turrets. The twin steel cupolas spun round and round searching for victims, their gunners obviously intent on keeping any attacker from the ground at the base of the bunker. Once there, the defenders knew, the attackers could use their explosives with impunity.

Next to Seagram the Piat operator aimed. He fired. The recoil was tremendous. The man yelped with pain as the weapon's padded butt slammed agonizingly into his shoulder. But the bottle-shaped bomb hurtled straight for its target. It slammed home just above the nearest slit, driving into the concrete and exploding with a tremendous roar. For a moment the whole bunker seemed to vibrate. Great chunks of concrete hurtled in every direction. The weapon which had been poking out of the slit buckled suddenly, as if it were made out of rubber, and then vanished as its owner fell to the ground inside the fortification.

Seagram didn't wait. 'Fire again!' he yelled at the groggy Piat gunner. 'Come on, lads.' Shouting and screaming terrible oaths, his little band streamed forward, trying to reach the dead ground near the bunker's walls, before the defenders could rally. Meanwhile the gunner fitted another bomb, shaking his head to clear it of the red and silver stars which were exploding like shells in front of his eyes.

But already the Germans were beginning to react. On the roof, the gunners depressed their machine guns as low as they could go and as the cupolas swung round and round, sprayed the ground around the bunker with a vicious hail of lethal fire.

Now Seagram's men started to take casualties. Here and there the piteous cry went up, 'Stretcher-bearers – I've bin hit!' But there were no stretcher-bearers coming. They'd survive or succumb on their own. As the infantrymen always quipped, 'There's only one way out of the infantry – *feet first!*'

The kid with the flame-thrower bobbing up and down on his back doubled past Seagram. He knew as soon as the German defenders recognized his weapon he'd be their prime target. Everyone hated flame-throwers. Now he dashed for the cover of a pile of cobbles some twenty yards from the rear entrance to the bunker. With hands that trembled badly, his chest heaving with the effort of his mad dash for cover, he pressed the trigger of his terrible weapon.

A soft hiss. The familiar whoosh. A long tongue of oil-tinged blue flame shot out viciously. It slapped against the bunker's rear entrance. It engulfed the steel door. The fiery embrace lasted a mere moment. Still, the heat was so tremendous that the concrete walls on either side glowed an ugly purple.

Immediately Seagram and the sapper sergeant changed direction. They could imagine the defenders trapped inside, clawing and jostling each other in their panic, frantically trying to escape that choking, all-consuming flame. They had to close with the defenders while they were still panicked.

Once more that terrible flame shot out of the flame thrower, the kid holding it standing there, legs apart, like some western gun-slinger in a Hollywood cowboy epic shooting it out with the bad guys. Again it wreathed the bunker in a glowing circle of fire. The camouflage paint started to bubble and boil and then burst, as if the concrete below it was alive. Abruptly the air was full of the acrid stench of burned paint.

'That's enough,' Seagram shouted.

The kid forced himself to take his finger off the trigger. The flame died down. Figures the like of which one would hope never to see in a lifetime began to stagger out of the bunker's side entrance. *'Kamerad,'* they cried piteously. 'Bitte, *Kamerad ... bitte.'* In front of them a couple dropped to their knees, wringing blackened claws for mercy, their uniforms and hair singed, crying and crying and crying. But not all gave in so easily. Behind the men on their knees, another bent swiftly and pulled something from his left jackboot. Even as Seagram recognized the object and shouted his warning, it was too late. *'Hell, grenade.'*

The kid, who had begun to vomit at the sight of his handiwork, reacted a second too slowly. The stick grenade exploded right at his feet. Even as he hurtled backwards with the force of the explosion, the fuel tank on his back burst into flame with a great whoosh. He shrieked. Greedily and instantly the flames shot up and wreathed his writhing body in their fiery embrace. Almost at once he began to burn. In seconds the kid's skull was transformed into a charred monstrosity. Where the eyes had been, there were two suppurating pits. For a moment he attempted to stay upright. To no avail. He fell to the ground, moaning in his acute agony as his bone burned away in a pool of blue oil.

The sergeant reacted first. He fired from the hip. A full burst of 9mm ammo from his Sten. The man who had thrown the grenade jumped back. Too late. His body disappeared into a thick red slurry that splashed and spattered the others trapped in the doorway. Next moment a burst from the cupola machine gun caught the sergeant. He went down, too, clawing the air frantically, as if he were attempting to climb the rungs of some invisible ladder.

In a flash, the situation was transformed. Now the German defenders knew that their attackers, what was left of Seagram's little force, were established at the base of the bunker. Sooner or later the Tommies would attempt to force their way inside using explosive charges and knock out the bunker. But until that happened they would take the first Englishmen attempting to get off the beach under fire and blow them to all hell.

It was something that Seagram knew too,

as he crouched there next to the dead sergeant who lay on his back staring at the cruel D-Day dawn sky with unseeing eyes. It was clear to the young naval officer that the fate of the South Lancs lay in his hands. The sergeant, who had been a very competent soldier, was dead; now he, Charlie Seagram, would have to make the military decisions, and he hadn't much time left to make them. The South Lancs would be moving into the attack at any time now. 'Christ Almighty, Charlie,' an angry little voice at the back of his brain exploded, 'you aren't an infantryman. What do you know of cracking open a concrete bunker? Give up, while there's still time to save yourself. Think of Lorna.'

He fought back against that persuasive voice. He told himself he couldn't think of himself now. The fate of the Iron Division's landing on this part of the beach lay in his hands. He couldn't consider himself, or even Lorna. His first duty was to King and Country.

'*King and Country!*' the little voice sneered cynically. 'What did King and Country ever do for you? A petty clerk's job in the City, a missus who whored around with the Yanks 'cos they had more money, and when you were on yer uppers, a drunk, they were ready to court-martial you at the drop of a hat. Bugger off with your bloody King and Country, pal!'

Seagram ignored the mocking voice. The country didn't owe him a living, he told himself, and there were thousands on this blood-soaked beach on this Tuesday who felt the same he did. England hadn't done much for them before the war and even during it their lives had been hard and frugal. Yet they were prepared to make the supreme sacrifice for a country that might well, in the end, prove as ungrateful as it had after World War One. But what did that matter?

Faintly through the vicious snap-and-crack of the infantry battle on the beach, Charlie Seagram heard the sound of the hunting horns. He knew what that meant. The officers of the South Lancs were waiting no longer; they were summoning their men to attack. Seagram knew he could not waste any more time. The bunker had to be taken, cost what it may, *now!*

Seagram rose from his crouched position. Huddled near the bunker's wall, with the devastating enemy fire zipping over their heads in a lethal noise, his survivors stared at him expectantly. They knew instinctively the officer held their fate in his hands. Now he would decide whether they would live or die. Sadly Seagram looked back at them. He had made his decision. The sound of the hunting horns was coming ever closer. 'All right, lads,' he said in a weary voice, 'we've got to give the PBI', he meant the Poor Bloody Infantry, 'a chance. Come on then ... let's get cracking. Good luck to you all...'

Then they were gone, swallowed up by the fog of war.

Six

There was still a sinister yet awe-inspiring majesty about the beach scene. The night shadows were already beginning to race across that shattered lunar landscape. The sky had become a startling electric blue. But the long streams of Allied bombers which stretched as far back as their bases in England were still visible in the dying sunlight, the planes' metal sides twinkling like fairy lights.

On the beach itself the long columns of tanks grinding up the heights and into the smoking ruins of the German defences made their way through the infantry, red-faced and sweating, laden like pack animals. Now there was none of the usual banter between tankers and footsloggers. They were all too tired; it had been a hard, bitter day. But they had broken through at last. Ahead of them lay the city of Caen, which General Montgomery had promised them they'd take this Tuesday.

Above them now the Pathfinders were dropping their great clusters of glittering flares and breaking slowly to the left as they finished doing so. The flares cascaded down in ever widening arcs like brilliant sparkling jewels. Puffballs of brown smoke rose above Caen. The German gunners were retaliating; they knew what was in store for them. In the tanks, the commanders closed their turret lids; they, too, knew what to expect soon. Violence and sudden death.

With great hollow booms, the first of the bombs started to land on the doomed French city. Great mushrooms of dark smoke began to ascend into the darkening sky to the east. The horizon erupted into a series of cherry-red fires. Slowly but surely the horizon was transformed. The night shadows fled. They were replaced by a great

crimson burning landscape that transformed the faces of the infantry into a glowing
unnatural red.

There was the hooting of a car in a hurry.
A ragged cheer flowed the length of the
infantry column. It was Montgomery's old
Rolls Royce, a Union Jack flying proudly at
its bonnet. 'Monty,' the infantry cried, their
weariness vanished for a moment. 'Good old
Monty!' The infantry weren't given to cheering generals, but Montgomery was different.

Standing bolt upright in the eerie red light,
Monty, the victor, saluted to left and right.
At regular intervals he threw out packets of
Woodbines. He didn't hold with cigarettes
himself, but he knew his soldiers kept going
on char and coffin nails. The Rolls moved
on, the driver still tooting his horn. The
battle of the beaches had been won. Monty
was on his way to supervise the new battle,
the one for the key city of Caen.

Grunting, the PBI plodded on. They filed
through the dead and the gaping shell holes.
The smell of death and decay was everywhere. Tanks and other armoured vehicles
lay drunkenly, knocked out everywhere,
their sides skewered, gleaming silver where
the German shells had penetrated. Clouds
of greedy flies buzzed around their open

turrets, waiting to feed on the dead inside the tanks.

A young naval officer as awed and as nervous as the infantry by this sombre scene of violent death, pushed his way through the soldiers. 'Ahoy there,' he called to his front, 'Ahoy there COPP party ... Ahoy...'

His call echoed and re-echoed among that ruined steel cemetery. There was no answer. The naval officer hesitated. He stood there perplexed, as if wondering what to do next. Somewhere to the rear in the growing darkness, a weary but angry voice called, 'Come on up there ... Get bloody moving will you?'

The young officer in navy-blue battledress tried again. He cupped his hands around his mouth and cried louder this time, 'COPP party, ahoy. Hello, are you there ... Answer, *please!*'

A hundred yards to his right, a solitary figure rose from behind a shattered wall. He stood there silhouetted a stark black against the flames now rising from the horizon. It was as if he had risen from the grave. He remained absolutely silent.

'COPP party?'

The figure still didn't answer. But to the left another rose – and another. One after another the handful of the survivors came

287

from their hiding places, now swaying violently, as if they might fall at any moment. The young officer's face blanched. It was as if he were rousing the ghosts of fighting men long dead. 'It's all right, chaps. It's all over now ... you can get back to the landing craft. Anyone seen Lieutenant Seagram?'

The first man to rise shook his head. Slowly he started to stagger towards the young officer sent by the Wizard. 'I say,' the officer said when the survivors came parallel with him. The soldier didn't seem to hear. The young naval officer's voice trailed away to nothing. He simply stared, saying nothing.

Looking like sleepwalkers, the survivors trailed by him in single file. They headed for the beach, glancing neither to left nor right. Mutely the young officer counted them as they did so. At ten he stopped counting and waited for more to emerge from their hiding places. None did. They were the only survivors. The price Seagram's force had paid for the shattered now silent bunker had been almost unbearably high in young men's lives. The battle was won. D-Day was over...